"I'm sorry.

There isn't an e̶...
I didn't want to...
It wasn't very pretty but she'd admitted the truth.

Ian's eyes widened. "Yer letter stated as such. I came to America to begin me new life. I am the third son, and as such I shall not inherit much land. In America I am able to have the land me sheep will need. Ye are not the only reason a man would…"

Hope gazed into his incredible blue eyes. They sparkled like sapphires. Hope swallowed. "I know I'm not doing this well but you have to understand, in America we pick our own spouses. And well, I don't…didn't… I guess I still don't like being told what to do. But I'm working on that." She paused for a moment, collected her thoughts and continued. "I hope you will forgive me for sending you the letter."

"Are ye wanting me to marry ye now?"

Lynn A. Coleman is an award-winning and bestselling author and the founder of American Christian Fiction Writers. She writes fiction full-time and loves visiting St. Augustine and other historical locations. She makes her home in Florida with her husband of forty years. Together they are blessed with three children (one in glory) and eight grandchildren.

Books by Lynn A. Coleman

Love Inspired Heartsong Presents

LYNN A. COLEMAN

The Shepherd's Betrothal

HEARTSONG
PRESENTS

Recycling programs for this product may not exist in your area.

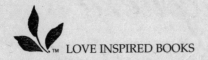 LOVE INSPIRED BOOKS

ISBN-13: 978-0-373-48771-4

The Shepherd's Betrothal

www.Harlequin.com

Printed in U.S.A.

Who can find a virtuous woman?
For her price is far above rubies.
—*Proverbs* 31:10

To Leanna

You're growing into a fine woman, and I'm proud of you. My prayer is that you continue to grow into the woman God has designed you to become. You are a kind, generous and strong young lady, and I love you.

Chapter 1

St. Augustine, Florida, 1871

Ian finished his breakfast at the Seaside Inn and pushed his plate away. He had a full day ahead of him, looking for land to raise his sheep on.

He had come to St. Augustine to break a betrothal arranged when he was five years old to fulfill an obligation his parents owed the girl's parents. He shook his head. All the worrying and praying he'd done had been for naught. His betrothed had sent him a letter breaking things off. It had arrived the day before he left for America. It made it easier not to have to explain his own reasons for wanting to break off the marriage, but it still left a bitter taste in his mouth. Would he still have left Ireland and come to America if he hadn't made all the arrangements before the letter arrived?

The innkeeper's wife came over to clear the table. "Ye made a fine breakfast again, Mrs. Arman, thank ye."

"You're welcome, Mr. McGrae," she replied with a smile, and headed off to the kitchen.

Ian had been staying at the Seaside Inn since his arrival in St. Augustine, three days now. He looked around in hopes of seeing the beautiful redhead who worked there. He'd noticed her when he'd checked in but hadn't seen her since. He wondered who she was.

He stood, deep in thought, turned toward the front door and slammed into the very woman who had so recently occupied his thoughts. "Forgive me, miss!"

She reeled back on her heels. Ian reached out and caught the poor woman. "I'm so sorry. I must have hit ye harder than I thought." Still holding the young lady up to keep her steady on her feet, he called, "Mrs. Arman?"

"What's the matter, Mr.— Hope, are you all right?"

"Hope?" Ian froze. Their gazes met, the shock in her eyes matching his own. "Hope Lang?"

Ian couldn't believe his ears or his eyes. Teetering in his embrace was the woman he'd been pledged to.

Her legs buckled. He scooped her in his arms and carried her to a chair. "I walked into her," he explained apologetically. "I must have hit her hard." He steadied her in the chair, concerned about her dazed look.

"You can let go of me now, Mr. McGrae."

Ian quickly removed his hands and stepped away from the two ladies. "Excuse me."

He bolted out of the inn. He didn't need to be around Hope Lang. He didn't need to be reminded of how this woman had been the thorn in his flesh for years. This was not how he had intended to meet the woman he'd been told since he was five years old he was going to marry; the woman who had sent a letter relieving him from his obligation. And yet there she was, a chambermaid, working at the very inn where he was staying.

Not to mention, she was beautiful.

He shook his head, confused by his own emotions. It wasn't like he hadn't wanted to be free from this burden his parents had put on him. He didn't want to be told who to marry, but he had saved enough to break the arrangement and pay off the debt. When she had written to break off their betrothal he had been relieved. But now... he wasn't sure what he was feeling.

Frustrated with himself, Ian stomped to the barn and retrieved his border collies. "Come," he snapped. Tara came, tail between her legs. She was the older of the two, her markings black and white with a patch over her left eye. Conall, two years younger, skulked warily behind her. His markings were brown and white with a patch over his right eye.

He bent down on one knee. "I'm sorry." The dogs nuzzled into his chest as he petted and reassured them. They were his only connection to home, to the life he'd left behind.

Except, in a strange way, for Hope. How could he be attracted to the woman he was no longer betrothed to? And how could they have met this way?

"Mr. McGrae," Richard Arman called out, cutting into Ian's thoughts. "Forgive me for intruding."

"Not at all," Ian responded, putting a polite smile on his face for the innkeeper. It would do little good to share his frustration. "What can I do for ye?"

"I'm uncertain as to what happened inside. Did you and Miss Lang have a disagreement?"

"Indeed no. Forgive me, I was simply startled by meeting Miss Lang in such a manner." Ian sighed. He stood up and scanned Richard Arman's face, then decided to change the subject. There was no need to inform others about his personal affairs. If Miss Lang wanted to tell her side of the story she was free to do so, but he would keep his own counsel. "The bank should have me funds today. I'll be settling me account."

"You are welcome to stay as long as you wish." Richard extended his hand.

Ian grasped the man's hand, amazed again that a man who worked behind a desk would have such strong and rugged hands. "Thank ye, I appreciate it. I am looking at another piece of land today."

"God's blessings on you." Richard walked back toward the inn.

"Conall, Tara, come."

The collies obediently kept pace as Ian walked down the street and headed toward the heart of St. Augustine. It was an interesting little city with its odd shops and Spanish architecture. By the time he reached the bank, the stroll had calmed him down. After his business at the bank was done, he headed out to see a piece of land for sale that might meet his needs.

While this one had more acreage, he wasn't as thrilled with the land as he had been with William Sanders's property, which he'd seen the day before. Sanders's lot seemed a much better fit for his needs—it had a river that ran along a third of the southern border, and it was only five miles from the city limits.

But did he even want to stay in the area? Would seeing Hope Lang ignite the anger he still felt about the betrothal? Anger he himself didn't entirely understand?

He headed toward the Sanders homestead, stopping only long enough to feed Conall and Tara. He knocked on the front door.

Mrs. Sanders greeted him. "Mr. McGrae, come on in."

"Thank ye." He turned to the dogs. "Stay," he instructed.

"Are these your sheepdogs?" Mrs. Sanders asked. She

was a round woman with short-cropped white hair and a twinkle in her eye that said she enjoyed life.

"Yes. Conall is two, Tara is four."

"They're handsome critters. Are they house-trained?"

"Yes, ma'am."

"Then come on in, Conall and Tara." The dogs sat in place. Mrs. Sanders gave Ian a questioning look.

"They only respond to me command."

"Oh, my gracious."

Ian gave a flick of his wrist and the dogs pranced into the house, not departing from his side.

"I was fixing myself some iced tea. May I fetch you some?" Mrs. Sanders led him to the rear of the house, into the kitchen.

"That'd be most kind of ye, thank ye. Is Mr. Sanders home?"

"Ring that triangle and he'll be here shortly."

A steel triangle and rod hung from a string outside the back door. Ian did as instructed.

He turned and found Mrs. Sanders chipping some ice off a block. "Where do ye get ice down here? I thought temperatures in Florida never hit freezing."

"Well, that's not exactly true. From time to time it gets cold enough to freeze. But ice is shipped down here from the north and stored."

Ian nodded. "One of the many things I will need to learn if I settle in Florida."

"That you will, son. Have a seat and make yourself comfortable."

"Thank ye."

She poured some water in a bowl and set it on the floor for the dogs. Ian gestured and both dogs drank.

"Mable, what's the trouble?" William Sanders came hurrying in with a hint of panic in his voice.

"No trouble at all, dear. Mr. McGrae has come to pay us another visit."

William Sanders smiled as relief washed over his face. Mr. Sanders had told Ian about her health concerns, and Ian thought that was why the old man wanted to sell his land.

Ian's mind drifted back to the frantic face of Hope Lang, and the way she had felt when he had picked her up in his arms. Instinctively he had wanted to protect her. But he had to stop thinking about Miss Lang. They were no longer betrothed.

"What can I do for you, Mr. McGrae?"

"I was wondering if Conall, Tara and I could walk the property. The dogs will give me a sense of the type of critters that I'll find."

"Of course. But I can tell you. We have the occasional wolf, bobcat, panther, coyote and sometimes even a Florida brown bear."

Ian sat back, surprised. "We don't have many predators in Ireland."

"Most of the land is fenced off with split rail and barbed wire. But as you saw, there are a few sections where you'd need to do some repair work."

"Yes, it would take some time to make the land ready for the sheep. I'll have to remove all the barbed wire and put in sheep fencing."

"Which brings me to a conversation I was having with Mable last night. We can lower the price a bit since we'll be keeping the house. Or we could lease the property to you for a year or two. Then you can purchase the land if you're happy with the place. And if not, you can simply move on."

Ian rubbed the stubble on his chin. "I shall prefer to purchase, and the lower price for not including the house and the land around it would be helpful, thank ye."

William and Ian discussed the details of the purchase and put some notes down on paper for the lawyer who would write out the agreement. Ian stood and offered his hand. "A gentleman's agreement then?" Ian couldn't believe he'd made the decision so quickly but the land felt right, and he would enjoy having the Sanderses as neighbors.

William gave Ian's hand a hearty shake. "Deal."

Mable smiled. "Wonderful. Will you be bringing a bride?" Mable asked.

Ian's mouth went dry. "If the Good Lord blesses, then perhaps one day."

"I'll be praying for you," Mable offered.

William slapped him on the back. "As will I. There isn't anything better than to have a good woman working at your side."

"Thank ye."

What else could he say? He certainly didn't want to tell the world about Hope Lang and his broken betrothal. His feelings were still a jumble. He'd been planning to break it off himself, and then she'd done it, which should have come as a relief, but now that he'd laid eyes on her, held her in his arms, something in him had shifted.

Why did he feel so rejected?

Somehow, Hope managed to get through her chores at the inn after her encounter with Ian McGrae. She'd been helping Grace Arman at the Seaside Inn as a favor to her best friend. Grace had not been feeling well and suspected she might be pregnant.

If only she hadn't lost her job with Hamilton Scott. It wasn't the perfect place to work but it was a good place to start in the business community. Even at a secretary level she was still learning about the inner workings of a business. However, the loss did allow her to help Grace out.

While working at the inn wasn't the type of work Hope preferred, she liked being useful. She had always prided herself on her ability to make good, sound decisions, which was why she'd done so well working for Hamilton Scott and his associates. Until he found fault with her work. Which still didn't make sense to her even these many days later.

Of course, of all the hotels in St. Augustine, Ian Mc-Grae had chosen to stay at the Seaside Inn. Hope had learned who he was the previous day and was planning to introduce herself and try to explain why she'd sent the letter.

With her responsibilities done for the day, she ran home, debating her next step. She felt it was still her duty to speak with Mr. McGrae and explain to him why she wrote the letter to break off their betrothal. But now she was wondering whether he'd even gotten the letter. If he had, why would he be here? If he hadn't, she would have to break it off face-to-face. Oh, could this get worse?

Hope's hands started to shake. Last night she had confessed to her parents that she'd sent the letter. They were not pleased but said they would not interfere with her decision.

Hope nibbled the inside of her cheek. She'd been hoping to receive a letter from Ian stating that he, too, wanted to end the betrothal. Instead he'd come to America.

Her mother walked into the kitchen. "Hope, may I have a word with ye?"

"Of course."

"Sit down." Her mother patted the seat of a chair next to the island in the center of the kitchen. Hope sat down and clasped her hands together. "Ye father and I would like you to know a bit more about why we accepted the betrothal of the McGraes with their son, Ian. We were betrothed in a similar fashion." Hope sat up straight.

"Ye father and I never gave it much thought because it was our way. But we have decided you'll marry whomever your heart, the Good Lord and parents approve of. Ye are an American. We can no longer live in the old ways. At the time, your father and Mr. McGrae thought it best, and Mr. McGrae owed your father in a way that money or words could never satisfy. But after our discussion your father and I have agreed that no such arrangement should have been set so long ago."

Hope glanced down at her lap then back up to her mother, who had the same green eyes she'd inherited. "Thank you, Mum. I'm going to speak with Mr. McGrae about why I sent the letter. I feel badly that he came all the way to America to marry me…"

"Leave it in the Good Lord's hands, darlin'." Her mother gave her a light embrace and went to the backyard to tend to her garden. For so long she'd been building up her resentment toward her parents for making this betrothal arrangement and now they were loving, forgiving and supporting her. *How could I have been so wrong for so long?*

She shook off her thoughts and remembered the man she'd hurt. Grace had shared that Mr. McGrae hadn't had American currency to purchase meals, and she suspected that he was getting by with only his breakfast for the day, so Hope had decided to pack him a sandwich. Making him dinner was the least she could do to show Christian charity toward him. She'd offended him. She couldn't say that she'd broken his heart, since he didn't know her. No, it was a matter of honor—a commitment to their parents that she'd broken.

She loaded the carriage with the basket of food and headed back to the Seaside Inn.

Ian walked into the backyard and headed for the barn as the sun melted in the west. She watched from the back porch as he looked after his dogs, noting his loving touch upon their heads as he settled them down for the night.

He stood about six inches taller than her own five foot two. He had a sleek, muscular build with brown hair and a square chin, with a short, well-trimmed beard. Earlier she'd noticed how blue his eyes were.

"Mr. McGrae, may I have a word with you?"

Ian turned, and his expression hardened. "What would ye like to say, Miss Lang?"

"I'm sorry you came to America. I had hoped you'd received a letter from me…" Hope trailed off uncomfortably.

Ian inhaled deeply and let the air out slowly, then simply nodded. Gone was the wondrous smile she'd seen on his face the previous day, before he knew who she was. "I did."

Hope stiffened, stunned. *Then why did you come?* She gathered her resolve and continued. "I would like to explain why I wrote the letter. Actually, I really would prefer not to explain…but I feel you are owed an explanation." Hope gave him the best smile she could muster and pointed to her basket. "I brought you something to eat. Grace said you haven't had American money and have been only eating breakfast, so…" She let her words trail off.

He looked down at the basket. "Me funds have been transferred into the bank now. Thank ye for the kind offer but I'm fine."

"May I explain?"

His eyelids slid down over his piercing blue eyes, then he nodded.

"There are a couple of sandwiches, some fruit, cookies and a pint of fresh milk to wash it all down. Please," she said, picking up the basket and offering it to him.

He accepted it as if it were infested, then extended his hand toward the yard with a forced politeness. "Where shall we sit?"

"There's a table and benches in the garden where Richard and Grace eat some of their meals."

"Very well."

Hope stepped forward toward the picnic table and gripped her sides. *God give me strength.* Ian treated his dogs graciously…but her, not so much. She couldn't blame him. "As I said, I wanted to apologize. I'm sorry, there isn't an easy way to put this other than I didn't want to marry you."

There, she'd said it. It wasn't very pretty but she'd admitted the truth. She had other dreams and desires, including falling in love with a man before she committed to live the rest of her life with him.

Ian gazed at her with those compelling eyes. "Ye letter stated as much. I came to America to begin me new life. I am the third son and as such I shall not inherit much land. In America I am able to have the land me sheep will need. I did not come for ye."

Hope swallowed, closed her eyes and calmed herself. "I know I'm not doing this well but you have to understand, in America we pick our own spouses." She opened her eyes. "And, well, I don't…didn't… I guess I don't like being told what to do." She paused for a moment, collected her thoughts and continued. "I hope you will forgive me for sending you such a letter."

Ian stared at the basket of food then glanced back at Hope. "Are ye wanting me to marry ye now?"

"No, of course not, no! I'm sorry. I only wanted you to know the truth. My parents didn't know that I'd sent you the letter, and after you arrived I told them, but this does not concern you."

"I am no longer bound to ye?"

"No, ye are not," she said, slipping into his brogue, the same as her parents'. "Sorry—you are not."

Ian smiled. "I trust ye will find a good man one day."

"Thank you, that is most kind. I never meant to hurt you."

Ian shook his head. "Ye did not hurt me."

Hope knitted her eyebrows. *Right, and it snows in Florida.* "What will you do now?"

"I purchased some land today. I'll be working on it for a while and then I'll purchase some sheep. I'm a shepherd."

"Whose land, if you don't mind me asking?"

"William Sanders's. It's a fine piece of land. It needs work but it has good grassland and roots to feed me livestock. Unfortunately, the agreement doesn't include a house. But the barns and outer buildings will be mine."

Hope relaxed. He was not as angry or as hurt as she'd expected him to be. "Are those sheepdogs?"

"Border collies. But yes, they work the sheep. Although the Irish sheepdog might do better in this Florida heat. They have less fur."

Hope stood up. "I'll let you eat your meal in peace. Again, I am sorry…"

He nodded. "Good day, Miss Lang."

She could feel the tension in the air between them, but she knew there was nothing else to say. "I'm happy you found some land. God's blessings on you, Mr. McGrae."

"And on ye, Miss Lang."

Hope stepped up into her carriage and drove off. A weight had been lifted.

So why did she still feel burdened?

Chapter 2

The boards in the wagon rattled. Ian slowed the horse down. A two-person buggy with a black canopy approached from the opposite direction, driven by a woman. Ian scooted over to the right. As the wagon drew closer he saw a crown of red hair. Ian's hands tightened on the reins. *Hope?*

It had been a couple of days since he last saw her. She was a rare beauty with her red hair, green eyes and porcelain skin. Ian couldn't understand his mixed emotions regarding Hope. She could have been his…but neither of them had wanted the betrothal. Not that he'd confessed his own desire to end it.

The oncoming carriage slowed to a stop alongside his. The woman was not Hope, but an older version of her. This could be none other than Mrs. Sally Lang.

"Good morning…Mr. McGrae?" Mrs. Lang greeted him with a wave and a smile. "Hope told me ye purchased the Sanderses' place."

"Good morning, Mrs. Lang?" He wanted to ask why she was out here. Was she trying to reactivate the betrothal?

"Aye, I did," he responded instead.

"It's a fine day." She glanced at the back end of his wagon. "Are ye buildin' something?"

"A room in the barn for a place to stay on me land."

"Aye, 'tis a good thing to be close to yer work. I've been out visiting with Rosemarie Hastings."

"I met her and her husband. They be kind folk."

"That they be, Mr. McGrae. I won't keep ye. Have a good day."

"And ye, Mrs. Lang." She jiggled the reins and the horse obeyed.

Ian turned and watched as she drove past. The Langs were a curious lot. Ian took the reins and commanded the horse forward. Why did Mrs. Lang's apparent ease at conversing with him bother him? After all, she didn't know that he had planned on breaking the betrothal, as well.

Father, I don't understand. Help me get past this. Help me figure out why I'm reacting with such feelings...

Back at the property, William Sanders came over and gave him a hand unloading the wagon. "The wife and I were wondering if you'd like to join us for dinner this evening."

"Thank ye, that is most kind, but I'll be working 'til the sun goes down."

"We can postpone dinner until then."

"Thank ye. A home-cooked meal would be appreciated. Thank yer wife, too, please."

William nodded. "What are you working on now?"

"I'm going to fashion a room of some sort in the barn so I won't need to keep paying room and board at the Seaside."

William Sanders nodded. "I'm sorry the house didn't come with the agreement."

"Ye gave me a fair price for the land without the house, I have no complaints. But I must be a wise servant with me funds. I shall not be making a profit for a couple of years, so I must be economical."

William smiled. "You are a smart young man. I wish I'd been as wise when I was your age. Good day, sir."

"Good day, and thank ye for the help." Ian went back to work unloading the wagon.

By the end of the day he had put his tools away, washed up and joined the Sanderses in their kitchen for a hearty fried chicken dinner.

"This be some of the best fried chicken I've ever eaten, Mrs. Sanders." In truth, he'd only had it once before, only just recently in St. Augustine. He was learning about the different foods in the area. "And these black-eyed peas… I've never had the like."

"Thank you, Mr. McGrae."

"Son, you'll have to try grits next."

Ian chuckled. "Mrs. Arman made some cheese grits this morning. They were all right."

William laughed. "I'm sure your mother had more ways to cook mutton and lamb than most of us do here."

"For certain." Ian wiped his mouth with his napkin. "If you'll forgive me, I must get back to the inn."

Mrs. Sanders smiled. "Thank you for visiting with us."

Ian stood to go. "Before you leave, may I ask you something?" William inquired.

"Yes, sir."

"Would you mind if we gathered a group to help you build the room in the barn?"

Ian cocked his head. "What do ye mean?"

"We'd host an event. We can plan a picnic. The men

will build. And the women will cook and sew up some curtains and bedding for you, as well."

Ian hesitated. A small room wouldn't take him too long on his own. On the other hand, he didn't want to insult the Sanderses by refusing their offer. He shifted his weight and Conall and Tara sat upright. "I don't believe I could afford to feed a large group."

"Nonsense, you don't pay for the food. Everyone chips in. You're the honored guest, and we'd come to support you."

Ian had heard of groups helping others build their homes, and he guessed this would be a similar event. He rubbed his chin. "I suppose it would be fine."

"Good! Then we'll plan it for this Saturday. In fact, if you have the funds for the materials, we could probably gather enough men to build you a small house rather than a room in the barn. Think on it, son."

Ian nodded. "I shall. Thank ye."

"Mable and I will take care of everything. You have the plans drawn up and the supplies here and everyone else will take care of the rest."

"Are ye certain?"

"That I am, son, that I am." William Sanders beamed.

Ian didn't know exactly what William was so happy about, but reasoned it gave the man pleasure to come to the aid of another.

Farewells expressed, Ian found himself walking back to the Seaside in the dark, his mind swirling with the generous offer. The dogs kept pace at his side. The moonlit sky bathed the white coral sands of the road in cotton-soft light. A contented sigh escaped his lips. "St. Augustine seems to be the right place for me after all, Lord." He wondered if Hope would be among those who would come to help.

* * *

Hope's family received word of the Saturday building party for Ian McGrae. Father and her brother Gabriel would be lending a hand, and she and her mother would work with the sewing circle and cook meals. Mrs. Sanders had arranged every detail. It seemed to Hope that Mr. McGrae had endeared himself to the elderly couple.

Friday night she and Gabe brought over some tables and chairs, as well as some concrete blocks and a steel grate for a grill top. The Hastingses were donating a side of beef and the cooking had already started early that morning.

The smell of slow-cooking meat filled the evening air. "I'll work all day for some of that barbecue," Gabe said.

"You will, brother." Hope chuckled as they got down from the wagon and started to unload the tables.

"Let me give ye a hand." Hope's back stiffened at the sound of a now familiar voice. "Miss Lang, why are ye here?" Ian asked, close enough now to see them clearly in the evening light, the edge in his voice unmistakable. Gabe glanced in her direction and watched as Mr. McGrae approached.

Hope swallowed her pride and remembered her manners. "Mr. McGrae, this is my brother, Gabe. You met him many years ago when you were young fellas in Ireland."

Last night her parents had shared the details of the arrangement with Ian McGrae's parents. His parents wanted to pay her parents for the food and supplies they'd given the McGraes when they left Ireland for America, so they suggested an arranged marriage between their children.

"Hello." Gabe extended his hand.

Ian shook the proffered hand and then went to the back of the wagon without offering to assist Hope down from the carriage. Instead, Gabe came to her rescue.

Hope walked over to the barbecue pit and smoker where her friend Mercy's older brother, Jack Hastings, was working. She needed distance from Mr. McGrae before she said something unsociable. "Smells great."

Jack stood up. "My stomach's already doing flips. It's good to see you, Hope."

"Thanks. I heard Mercy and the baby are doing well."

Jack smiled. "They are. They'll be coming next month for a couple of weeks."

"Your parents must be so excited."

Jack chuckled. "Yes, but my wife is due next month so Mother will have her hands full. Speaking of which, I'm wondering if you might lend me a hand. I'd love to surprise Diane with a new dress after the baby is born."

"I'd be happy to help."

"Next time I'm in town I'll leave some money at the mercantile for you to purchase whatever you need."

Hope smiled. "Your mother must be beside herself." She knew how much Rosemarie Hastings loved her grandchildren. She wondered if her mother would have the joy of having grandchildren one day. Gabe didn't seem to be interested in seeking out a wife anytime soon, and she certainly wouldn't be getting married for a while, seeing as how she was planning to marry a man she loved. Love took time, or so she guessed.

She watched as Gabe and Ian brought the tables over toward a clearing illuminated by lanterns. "Has Mr. Mc-Grae decided if he's building a house or a room in the barn?" she asked Jack.

"A small house. Room enough for a bed, sitting room and small kitchen."

Hope nodded.

"May I have a word with ye, Miss Lang?" Ian asked as he and Gabe came toward the fire.

"Yes, sir." Hope stepped toward Ian, wondering nervously what he could possibly want to talk about.

He escorted her back to the wagon. "I must ask ye for forgiveness. I spoke harshly with ye when ye arrived and I must apologize."

Hope nodded. "I understand."

"I appreciate yer forgiveness but I do question me behavior. It was not right, and I seem to say everything with an edge when I see ye. I am sorry. And I will try to refrain from such poor behavior in the future."

She reached out to lay a comforting hand on his forearm, but thought better of it. "You are forgiven, Mr. Mc-Grae. I hope one day you will forgive me."

Ian rubbed the back of his neck. "Perhaps that *is* me problem. I shall pray about it during me evenin' prayers."

"Get some rest, Mr. McGrae. Tomorrow will be a long, hard day but it will produce so much blessing."

Ian smiled, and his blue eyes flashed in the lamplight. A woman could get lost in those eyes. If only he didn't look at her with such…what? Contempt? No, disapproval, disappointment even. The wound in Ian Mc-Grae ran deep.

"Good night, Miss Lang."

Gabe came up. "Ready?"

"Ready."

"I'll see you at dawn tomorrow morning," Gabe said to Ian as Hope climbed up into the wagon.

Father, give me strength to get through tomorrow. Hope wondered how many of her friends knew of her breaking off her betrothal to Mr. Ian McGrae. Then again, how many even knew she'd been betrothed? She'd kept that a secret from just about everyone. *Once the single ladies of St. Augustine get their eyes on him,* she told herself, *he'll find a spouse without much trouble at all. Perhaps then he'll be able to forgive me, Lord.*

Chapter 3

Hope tried to rest and utterly failed. Most of the night she found herself tossing and turning. She'd even gotten up once or twice and gone to the kitchen. Why did she bring out such anger in Ian McGrae? Of course, that was a foolish question. She knew why.

What could she do to not irritate him anymore? Yes, he had apologized, which only showed that she really had offended him.

She'd gone back and forth all night as to whether or not to attend the building party. Perhaps it would be best if she stayed home. Her parents would understand. At least she hoped they would understand. Hadn't she brought enough grief into Ian McGrae's life already?

Hope moaned and rolled over into her pillow. The sun would be rising in an hour. Her father and brother would be leaving at that time. She and her mother did not have to arrive until a couple of hours later. Several of the women were talking about quilting a blanket for Mr. McGrae. While she had helped with quilting in the past, it felt too intimate of a project to be a part of with regard to Ian McGrae.

At last, the weariness of the hour took over and she fell into the deep sleep of exhaustion.

Later, the gentle touch of her mother's hand on her shoulder stirred her. "Mother, what time is it?"

"Ten o'clock."

"Oh, dear. I'm sorry, I overslept."

Her mother laughed. "Darlin', ye more than overslept. This is the second time I've tried to wake ye. Care to tell me what kept ye up most of the night? I heard ye in the kitchen."

"I'm sorry. Did I wake you?"

"A little, but that's the way of a mum. So tell me, what be on your mind?"

"Ian."

"Ah, ye fancy him then?"

"No, not that," Hope insisted a bit too quickly. "Well, he is rather handsome. But that isn't the problem. Well, maybe a little. No, it has to do with these emotions I evoke in him. His words were cutting and harsh when he first spoke to me. Not that I blame him. After all, he did come all the way from Ireland and...well, you know. Now it seems he can't be near me without getting angry or upset."

"Ah. Well, there is only one thing ye can do and that is to be full of grace and compassion when he is angry. Turn the cheek, as the Bible says. If he be a good Christian man he'll give his feelings to the Good Lord to handle."

"But Mum, how can he forgive me? I was horrible to him, to you, to Father."

Her mother took her hand. "Hope, ye need to forgive yourself before ye can expect anyone else to forgive ye."

"I know you are right." Hope shook her head. "I thought I was making the right decision. But the fact that I hid that I wrote the letter shows that I knew it was wrong."

Her mother paused, looked down at her hands then back at Hope. "Love is a difficult thing. There is the high excitement of passion, and that is good in its proper place. But, like we read in the Bible, 'charity suffereth long, and is kind…it doth not behave itself unseemly.' Ye need to love thyself, Hope, and trust in God's forgiveness for not discussing your desires to break off the betrothal. You know yer father and I forgive ye, but ye need to forgive yourself."

Hope closed her eyes. "You are right, Mum. Thank you."

"Ye are welcome. Now, I must return to the building party. Ye are welcome to come or stay at home."

"Give me a moment to get ready."

Her mother smiled. "I'll be downstairs."

When they drove up to Ian McGrae's new property and secured the horse and buggy away from the work site, Hope saw that the men already had the walls up on the small house and some of the roof done. Windows, doors and shingles still had to be completed. By Hope's estimate there were probably a couple dozen men working.

"Welcome back, Sally. It is good to see you, Hope." Mrs. Sanders welcomed them as they joined the ladies, sewing needles and thimbles in hand. Most of the design side of the quilt was done. A few ladies had begun working on some curtains.

"Are the men stopping for lunch?" Hope asked.

"Only long enough to grab a sandwich or two," Mrs.

Sanders explained. "The sandwiches are all made and in that box on the table. That barrel is full of sweet tea and ice. The other barrel is full of ice water. Dinner is planned for sunset. I'm glad you could join us, Hope."

"Pleasure to lend a hand." Hope glanced over at Grace, who winked back at her. Grace understood the inner turmoil she wrestled with. Grace, too, had tried to convince Hope to forgive herself and allow God's forgiveness to flow. But Hope hadn't listened. If she had, perhaps she would have slept last night, something to write in her journal.

Her mother's words rang true—it was she who needed to forgive herself. She hadn't broken Ian McGrae's heart. Just then, she glanced over at the house and saw Ian standing on the center beam of the roof. "Is he crazy?" Her own heart did a somersault. Of course, Ian McGrae was not hers to worry about.

Ian glanced over to the ladies' sewing circle. Hope and her mother had joined in. Apparently he hadn't offended her too much. At least she'd come.

Ian was enjoying getting to know some of the men of the community as they worked together on the house. He especially enjoyed getting to know Gabe and Mr. Lang. Gabe was his age but otherwise they were totally different men. Gabe liked working in commerce. Ian liked working with livestock and the land.

Ian balanced himself on the ridge beam of the roof and walked to the other end of the house. The men suggested that he angle the house so that the east-west winds would blow through and cool it down in the summer months.

Ian stood on the southern peak of the roof and scanned the ranch he had just purchased. The rich, green pasture was broken by occasional patches of brown hay and sea oats blowing in the wind. A river flowed lazily along-side it, bending with the roll of the land and providing water for his livestock…the livestock he didn't have yet.

"What you looking at?" Gabe asked.

"Just taking in the view. It's a prime piece of property."

"I believe you're right. If Mr. Sanders didn't have health issues, it would be full of cattle right now."

Ian stepped off the ridge beam onto the roof slats. "What health issues?" So Mr. Sanders had health prob-lems along with his wife.

"Don't rightly know. But I do know that he had to sell his stock a couple of years back, and now the land. He has aged quickly since then. My father always says if a man doesn't have his work he can wither like a blade of grass in the Florida sun." Gabe grabbed a pocket full of nails and climbed up the ladder to join Ian on the roof. "Get a move on, we haven't got all day."

Ian chuckled. "Aye, Captain."

Harvey Gage poked his head out the window of the kitchen. "Hey, that's my rank." Gage was a retired sea captain and a friend of Manny's, another resident of the Seaside Inn. Richard and Grace Arman treated him like an uncle, though they were not related. "Manny and I are building a cupboard in the kitchen for you to store some food, plates and other things in. Do you want the sink under the window?"

"That would be nice, thank ye."

Manny appeared next to Harvey. "Sounds like a good place for it." He scratched his hat and beamed his tooth-less grin.

Ian still could not believe all the work they'd accom-plished so far today. He grabbed a couple of boards and worked his way across the roof, nailing them in place. Five other men were also working on the roof. "Planning to get the felt on in an hour, better get a move on, Ian," Richard called out.

"Yes, sir." Ian climbed down and handed up five more planks. He glanced at the bundles of cedar shingles. No doubt about it, they'd have this roof ready in an hour.

In addition to Ian's plans the men had added a covered porch on the east and west sides, a benefit in the Florida sun. They had raised the house three feet off the ground, letting him know it would help with the airflow, keeping the house cooler. Unlike in Ireland, where the foundation went belowground at least three feet to keep the surface temperatures from cracking the foundation.

An hour before sunset, the sky was beginning to turn orange and pink. The men stood back and examined their work. "It's a sound house, Ian," William proclaimed.

"Thank ye all for all the help. I never would have been able to accomplish so much alone."

"Pleasure to help. Now," Jackson Hastings, Jack's father, began, "I for one am ready to take a dip in that river before I eat. Anyone joining me?"

"We'll have dinner ready when you come back," one of the ladies shouted.

At that, the men went down to the river. They found a spot behind the trees, took off their outer layers and dived in. Ian floated to the surface, turned onto his back and let the gentle stream float him downriver.

For the first time since his arrival in America, he felt at peace.

Until Gabe "cannonballed" him. The two wrestled in the water, laughing and struggling for the advantage. The others cheered them on as they wrangled back and forth, splashing, sputtering and coughing, but neither giving in to the other. Finally, Ian got the jump on Gabe and dunked him to the bottom. Ian jumped up, raising his arms in victory. Gabe sputtered to the surface, laughing, as he choked out the words "You got me."

"Aye, but I've had a bit more practice I think with two older brothers and one younger. We've wrestled a time or two. The hook in me nose came from one of our matches. I'm proud to say I won, but it did cost me me good looks."

"He's got a bit of the blarney in him," Drake Lang, Hope's father, proclaimed.

All the men joined in the laughter.

"Aye, that be true," Ian admitted.

As they worked their way toward shore, Ian noticed a wheelbarrow full of towels. The Sanderses certainly knew how to organize a building party.

After they were dried and dressed the men made their way back to the cooking area. The only man who had stayed behind was Jack, taking care of the meat in the smoker and roasting on the pit. "If you don't mind, Dad, I'll let you finish the steaks and burgers and I'll take a quick dip."

"Be happy to." Jackson took his son's place and Jack ran down to the river.

Ian scanned the area. The tables were separated and planks placed between them to extend their length. The volume of food filled all three tables. Plates and utensils had been provided by the different families. Ian felt a lump rise in his throat. "Ye ladies have honored me, thank ye. Thank ye all so very much."

Just then, he turned to see Hope walking out of his new house. A lamp or candle was lit inside and the soft glow made the house appear warm and inviting. Had she done that for him? Ian shook his head, lost in emotion. "I don't know what to say."

William came up and slapped him on the back. "'Thank you' is all that is needed. Everyone here likes an excuse to get together and eat. Mable and I thank all of you, as well. Reverend, would you say the blessing?"

The reverend wasn't wearing a cleric's robe today. He'd arrived about midday in overalls and had pounded nails with the rest of them. "Father, we ask your blessings on Mr. McGrae and his new home and property. We ask that You prosper him and his undertakings. Guide him in Your ways, Lord, and bless him with an abundance of Your mercy, grace and hope. In Jesus's name, amen."

A round of amens and cheers went up from the entire group. Ian planted his feet and tried to control the emotions roiling inside him.

Mable came up beside him. "The ladies put together a little gift for you. It's in your house. You can take a look later." She winked.

"Thank ye, Mrs. Sanders." Ian reached out and embraced her as if she were his own grandmum. "Thank ye very much." He looked up…into Hope Lang's eyes.

Hope's eyes teared up, seeing the genuine affection Ian showed for Mrs. Sanders. The woman was a marvel. She'd been rounding up items for Ian's home for the past three days. He had more furnishings than most in their first homes.

The afternoon swim had been orchestrated so the ladies could move all of Ian's new belongings into place. Grace and Richard had brought the crate Ian had stored in the Seaside Inn's barn. Others brought plates, cups, silverware, pots, pans, a bed, a small table and a couple of chairs, plus an overstuffed chair in the corner for comfort and reading. There was a chest of drawers, and Manny and Harvey had not only built a cupboard but a small closet, as well. The curtains and bedspread were new, all made that day by the ladies.

Hope stood in line and worked her way down the table. Jackson's barbecued ribs were the highlight of the meal and she doubted there would be any left over. The roast beef with finger-licking sauce was her next choice. There were steaks and hamburgers, not to mention all the pork, and an abundance of corn bread, baked beans, coleslaw, fresh vegetables and rolls. The last table was filled with pies, cakes and other sweets.

A fire was lit in the center of the eating area, and Harvey pulled out a fiddle and started to play. It was a grand evening at the end of a wonderful day. Hope couldn't be more proud of her family, neighbors and church friends. She watched as Ian ate and then made his way around the circle thanking everyone individually.

She got up and left her seat when he was three people away from her. There was no sense ruining his day. She didn't want to bring out his anger.

When she returned he had worked his way around the circle and was sitting and enjoying his meal. Every now and again she would catch his gaze and before she had the time to look away he would narrow his on her, leaving an unsettling feeling in the pit of her stomach.

By nine o'clock families were packing their wagons. Hope grabbed her parents' contribution to the meal, or rather the empty containers from their contributions.

"Hope!" her mother called.

She joined her family as they prepared to leave and sat beside her mother. Her father and brother stood on the back of the carriage. As they were about to leave, Ian popped his head in the buggy. "I'm glad I caught ye. I just wanted to say thank ye, Miss Lang, for all yer help today."

"You're welcome, Mr. McGrae." His face was so alive and happy. She hadn't realized that such a joyous smile was hiding under all those scowls he gave her. Perhaps they could find harmony living in the same town after all.

Ian leaned back and tapped the top of the carriage. "Good night and God bless ye."

Her mother directed the horses to trot behind the others in the departing caravan. The lanterns lit a dim, golden path down the road.

"How are ye?" her mother whispered.

"Good, thank you, Mum."

"Perhaps tonight ye can get some sleep."

Hope giggled. "And you."

"Aye, and me, as well." Her mother winked.

How could she have had such negative thoughts about her parents for so long? Pride and arrogance, she guessed. *Dear Lord, there is so much I need to change.*

Ian watched as the departing carriages and wagons bounced down the road toward the city. He turned and looked at his new home. His heart tightened in his chest. He didn't deserve such favor. Especially from the Langs. He'd been short with Hope, and less than generous. And yet she and the rest of the family had turned out to help him. Ian shook his head and decided it was time to see his new home from the inside.

He whistled for Conall and Tara. The two came to his side. "Let's go see our new home," he said.

He stepped up onto the porch. The low roof overhead was angled to shade the windows from too much sunlight and too much heat. He'd learned so much today about Florida—the heat, the winds, about cooling the house. They'd told him to plant trees around the house for added shade and protection. He was grateful he'd chosen the riverfront property, and could take a quick dip in such refreshing, cool water whenever he liked.

When he opened the door, he staggered back on his heels, marveling at all the work the ladies had done on his behalf. He found a note on the table.

Dear Mr. McGrae,
These items are all extras from our homes that we thought you could use.
      The quilt and curtains were made by the ladies today, everything else came from our surplus.
      God bless you,
Your neighbors.

Ian stumbled into a nearby chair and read the note one more time. Tears came to his eyes. He was so undeserving of this. And yet the Good Lord blessed him anyway.

His hands started to shake. He missed his family, his home, and yet he'd come to a strange land and had been blessed by meeting just the right people. No man would count that a coincidence. God had been meeting his needs long before he knew what his needs were. His parents' prayers had been answered. His prayers had been answered.

And yet there was a knot in his stomach. He had allowed Hope to believe she was the only one responsible for breaking their betrothal. If she hadn't sent that letter first, he would have been the one disappointing her parents, possibly even Hope herself. He understood her reasoning, but he'd kept his secret from her and from her family. Why had he done that? To punish her for hurting him?

He fell to his knees and cried out to the Lord. "Dear God, I don't deserve any of this." He prayed and repented. For over an hour he opened his heart to the Lord, then finally got up, exhausted both physically and spiritually. He readied himself for bed and slipped between the sheets.

The next morning, he dressed and got ready for church. "Come, Conall and Tara, we'll be going to church today."

On the walk to town, he passed the Catholic church. Most Irish, he knew, were expected to be Catholic. He and his family, however, were Protestant. He had attended the Armans' church the first Sunday in St. Augustine. Today he was going to visit another. On the other hand, several of the folks who'd helped out yesterday came from the same church as the Armans, including the Sanderses.

Ian paused in the road. *Where should I go, Lord?* He continued on, undecided. He worked his way through the city streets and found himself back at the same church as the Sunday before.

The pastor greeted him at the door. "Good to see you, Mr. McGrae. That was quite a building party yesterday."

"Yes, it was, Reverend. Thank ye again for yer help."

"My pleasure. It is good to have you join us this morning."

Ian ordered the dogs to stay outside under the shade of a shrub and stepped inside. He admired the large stained glass windows as he sat down on a wooden pew toward the rear of the building. He bowed his head and prayed.

A few minutes later the service began in much the same fashion as it had the week before. The congregation sang with hearty voices and Ian found a deeper joy in singing this morning. He felt freer than he'd felt in years. It was hard to believe the toll his betrothal had taken on his life. He'd been walking around with a chip on his shoulder. He'd been angry with his parents for binding him to such a thing. He'd been angry at having no say in his future. Today, this morning, he felt free from that anger. He smiled at the simple awareness of the fact.

The service ended and Ian engaged in conversations with many of the folks who'd come to lend a hand yesterday.

"Good to see you, Ian," said John Samuels.

Ian reached out and gave him a hearty handshake, then pulled him in for a hug. "Thank ye again, John, I am overwhelmed."

"Pleasure to help." John's wife and children came up beside him. "Remember, I'm a tanner and if you need any help, just let me know."

"Thank ye, again, John. I will."

The same conversation was repeated again and again but Ian didn't tire of thanking everyone. In his peripheral vision he caught sight of Hope's crimson crown, accented by a white-laced hat displaying all the high fashion of a woman of society. Why was she chambering rooms at the Seaside Inn? Why would her father allow such a thing? And why would they betroth their daughter to a poor shepherd?

The Lang family was a bit of a mystery.

Hope glanced over and gave him a slight nod of recognition. It occurred to him that perhaps she'd sent him that letter because she didn't believe he was worthy of her affections. She raised her eyebrow. Her green eyes sparkled for a moment then she turned her focus to another— a man with broad shoulders and impeccable clothing, complete with a top hat and suit coat.

Ian exited the church. Why did it bother him if she was interested in another? She wasn't bound to him. And that was what he'd wanted, wasn't it? But the idea that a life with Hope would not have been a bad thing kept nagging at him. And for some unexplained reason, seeing her with another man did not sit well.

Chapter 4

Hope saw the disapproval in Ian's eyes, but she did not have time to think about that now. She turned her attention back to the man before her. "Thank you, David. I'll speak with my father and mention your interest."

"You are most kind, Miss Lang."

Dorothy, David's wife, came up beside him. "When is the baby due, Dorothy?"

"April. But Dr. Peck believes there may be two."

Hope smiled. "That's wonderful, isn't it?"

David chuckled. "Yes, but it does mean two of everything, which is why I'm hoping your father might be willing to invest—"

Dorothy lightly slapped his arm. "It's the Lord's day, sweetheart."

"Pardon me. You are right, Dorothy, as always."

Dorothy giggled and leaned closer to whisper in Hope's ear. "He doesn't really believe that but he knows it will keep me from arguing with him further."

Hope laughed. It was good to see folks who truly loved one another. She excused herself and headed out of the church. The sun was high in the sky. Hope shaded her eyes.

"Miss Lang." Hope turned to see Manny running toward her. "Miss Lang, Richard asked me to come find you. Grace is indisposed and we need some help at the inn."

Her mind raced. Knowing the delicate condition her good friend was in… "Of course. Let me tell my family and I'll be right there."

"Did you see Dr. Peck in the service this morning?"

"Dr. Peck? No. Is Grace sick?"

"Very."

Hope scanned the crowd and found Gabe. "Gabe," she called and waved. "Would you tell Mother and Father I need to help Grace? She's fallen ill. And could you also ask Mother to grab a couple of work dresses and some nightclothes for me? It might be prudent to spend the night. I don't know how serious it is but they're calling Dr. Peck."

"Absolutely. Is there anything I can do?" Gabe asked.

"No, not yet. Just bring me the clothes and I'll let you know then. Thank you." Hope lifted her skirt and ran toward the Seaside Inn. She knew it wasn't proper, but something was seriously wrong if they needed help and they needed the doctor. Richard was quite capable of taking care of the inn's chores. He'd been doing it for years.

Hope rounded the corner to the inn. She ran straight to Grace's bedroom door, where she paused and caught her breath before lifting her hand to knock. "Grace, it's me, Hope. May I come in?"

Richard opened the door. "Hope, thank you for coming."

"What's the matter?"

"We're not sure but she might have lost the baby."

Hope looked over at Grace. "I'm so sorry. What can I do?"

"The rooms need cleaning and I don't want to leave her side," Richard said.

She could see the fear in his eyes. "Of course not."

"You're the only one I could think of. You know what to do and how to do it. I'll take care of breakfast tomorrow morning but—"

"Richard. I'm happy to help." Hope stepped into the room. "Can I get you a cup of tea, Grace?"

"Tea would be nice, thank you." Her friend looked pale.

"I'm so sorry." Hope leaned over and kissed Grace's forehead. "I'll do whatever it takes."

"Thank you. I know you were planning on finding another office job this week but…"

"Do not worry. I can clean rooms and change sheets with the best of them," she said, trying to lighten the mood. It would only make Grace feel more guilty if she knew Hope had an appointment tomorrow morning for a job interview. She would write a note to be messengered over to Mr. Davis to cancel her appointment. "Let me go make that tea for you. What about you, Richard, can I get you something?"

"No, I'm fine."

"Go sit down with your wife before you fall down." Richard gave her a halfhearted smile. "Is there a room available tonight?" she asked.

"Room one, why?"

"Because I'll be spending the night." Hope placed her hands on her hips and challenged them to refuse her offer. Richard raised his hands in surrender and Grace smiled.

Hope went into the kitchen, lit the stove and started to heat up some water for tea. Here was another good reason to have broken her betrothal. She wouldn't be free to help her friend if she was newly married or in the midst of planning her wedding. She grabbed a tall glass and filled it with ice for Richard. She poked through the pantry and found some crackers and dried biscuits. She'd heard they were helpful for women in Grace's condition.

Tea made, she placed the items on the tray and headed toward their room. She knocked lightly and opened the door, finding them holding hands. Hope's heart ached within her over their possible loss. She placed the tray on the bedside table.

The bell over the front door jangled. "I'll take care of whoever it is," she offered.

"Thank you, Hope," Richard and Grace said in unison.

She went to the front desk and found her mother. "What's happening with Grace?"

Hope leaned over and whispered in her mother's ear, "She may have lost the baby."

"Oh, dear. I'll let Helen know. A gal needs her mother during times like this."

Something in her mother's eyes made Hope ask, "Mum? Did you lose a baby?"

"Yes, dear," she answered, handing over a small bundle of clothes. "But this is not the time or place to discuss such matters. Here are your work dresses and unmentionables. Send a message if ye need more. I'll come by tomorrow and check on Grace. Let her know she'll be in our prayers."

"Thanks, Mum." Hope reached over and embraced her. She was happy to have her own mother beside her. They could have been very upset with her breaking the betrothal; instead they'd accepted her decision and con-

tinued to love her in spite of her actions and behavior.
"I love you."

"I love ye, too, darlin'." Her mother kissed her cheek.
"I'll see ye tomorrow."

Ian rubbed the back of his neck. Why was he so judg-
mental concerning Hope? What did it matter that he'd
seen her at church speaking with a refined individual?
She was no longer committed to him, and that was the
answer to his prayer.

Admit it, he said to himself, *ye are attracted to the
lady.*

Ian found himself back on his knees repenting again
for his behavior. *Lord, why is it so hard? Why do I keep
falling into the same snare?*

He changed from his Sunday clothes and put on his
work clothes. He would need to paint the house, but first
there was a lot to clean up from the building party.

Outside, he began clearing the ground, picking up
scraps of wood and stacking them in a pile. They'd make
good starter fuel for his fires. His next purchase would
be a small stove and oven that would also heat the house
in the winter.

His thoughts were interrupted by the sound of approaching horse hooves.

"Hello!" Gabe Lang called out as he swung down from
his horse. "How'd it feel to sleep in your own place last
night?"

Ian smiled. "Wonderful. What can I help ye with?"

"Nothing, I came to see if you needed a hand."

"Don't need the help but a friendly conversation is
always welcome."

"Good." Gabe slapped him on the back. "'Cause I
would like to speak to you about my sister."

"Oh?"

"I notice things most people don't see. And you, my friend, were less than a gentleman to her when we delivered the tables on Friday evening."

Ian started to protest.

"Let me speak. I understand she hurt you. But try to see it from her point of view."

"I do, actually. She explained it to me."

"Oh. Well, then why have you been so…"

"Rude?" Ian supplied. "I don't know. Truth be told, I came to break the betrothal meself."

Gabe leaned back on his heels.

"Come," Ian said with a gesture toward the house. "Ye might as well know the whole truth of it." He wasn't sure why he wanted to confess to Gabe. Maybe because Gabe was so easy to talk to. Or maybe because he was just so tired of mulling it over all by himself.

Ian and Gabe sat down on the front porch and dangled their feet over the edge. "Me parents didn't tell me that I was betrothed to Hope for a debt to yer father until I was twenty-one. I began to work for extra income to pay off me father's debt so as not to have to marry. I prayed for years that God would work it out so that I wouldn't be obligated. Finally, I had enough money, and I had grown so hardened to the idea that me parents would use me as collateral…" Ian looked off in the distance. "Father sat me down and explained how your father had given them so much before they came to America. It was during a very poor season in Ireland and yer parents gave them all their food stocks and a few extra sheep. Then me father sold off a section of the land I would inherit one day and gave me the money and his blessing to break off the betrothal. This is what I came to do. I received yer sister's letter the day before I left for America. It was an answer to me prayers."

Gabe sat up straight, as if he were about to protest.

Ian raised a hand to stop him. "But I still felt betrayed. Why that is escapes me. I've prayed. I spent a good part of the evenin' after all of ye left last night on me knees. Then I see yer sister in church this morning speaking to a man dressed in fine clothes and realize she's meant to have a man from a better social class than I..."

Gabe chuckled. "It's my turn now. It's true, Hope felt similar resentment about the arranged betrothal. What she didn't know was that our parents had also had an arranged marriage. And they knew your parents and felt that you would be raised in a sound manner and would provide well for a wife. More than that, as Father has often impressed upon me, they believed you would be raised to treat a woman with respect and honor in a way that would please God.

"And what you probably don't know is that my parents didn't want to be paid back for the debt. Which means they didn't see this betrothal as the payment of a debt, but rather a security for their daughter's future."

Ian hid his surprise. "I don't believe I would have been a good man for yer sister."

Gabe smiled. "No, probably not. But she's my sister and I think she's special. I love her, and there is a right man out there. But as Father says, when you find a woman you can love more than yourself, she's the one to set your heart on."

"Yer father is a wise man."

"He is, but don't tell him I think so." Gabe chuckled.

"I should go and apologize to yer sister again." Ian jumped up.

"She's not home. She's at the Seaside. Grace is very sick."

"What? What happened? She looked fine last night."

"I couldn't tell you. Mother said 'female issues.'"

"Ah, I won't ask."

"Good, 'cause I stay clear of those kinds of issues. Now let's get some work done before the sun sets."

"Thank ye, Gabe. You've been like a brother to me, and ye are certainly a good brother to yer sister."

"I'm glad you think so, because this is your last warning. If you do anything to hurt my sister again..." Gabe paused. "I'll have to straighten that bend in your nose." Gabe chuckled and slapped him on the back. "We would have had fun growing up together as young fellas in Ireland."

And Ian felt it, too. How their lives would have been different if they'd grown up together.

A flash of Hope's poised beauty flickered in his mind's eye. If she had grown up in Ireland he would have sought her out as a mate. Perhaps that is what was bothering him, the fact that—given his own choice—he would have pursued a relationship with Hope. Gabe was right to admonish him and right to stand up for his sister. She was far too precious to be treated the way he'd treated her.

Gabe left as the sun was setting. Ian returned to his house and changed into clean clothes. His conversation with Gabe about Hope replayed in his mind. Determined to not let another day end without admitting his own desires to end the engagement, he whistled for the dogs and headed toward the Seaside Inn.

Hope sat in the library with her legs curled under her in one of the comfy reading chairs. Grace was doing well and the doctor said she might not have lost the baby after all. However, she would need to stay in bed for a week or so.

Hope had promised her time to Grace and Richard for as long as it took for Grace and the baby to be out of danger. Which would mean amending her note to Mr. Davis to let him know she wouldn't be available to interview for the position in his office.

The bell over the front door rang as someone let themselves in. She had put up the sign stating there were no more rooms for the night, so she stayed seated with her book. It was probably one of the other boarders returning from dinner.

Then the bell at the desk chimed. Grace slid a bookmark between the pages and went to the front desk. She was shocked when she saw Ian McGrae standing there with a bouquet of freshly cut flowers.

"Good evening, Miss Lang. I heard Mrs. Arman wasn't feeling well and thought I'd give her these." He handed the flowers to Hope. She relaxed.

"Thank you. I'll put them in water for her."

Ian nodded. "And I was hoping I could have a word with ye."

Hope stiffened. She couldn't imagine what he might want to discuss. "All right," she agreed. "You can meet me in the library. I'll take care of these and join you in a couple of minutes."

Ian walked toward the library as Hope headed in the opposite direction toward the kitchen. She fished out a vase and filled it with water. With slow, deliberate movements, she set the flowers in place and wiped her hands on a cloth. *Stop stalling and speak with him*, she inwardly chided herself.

Ian stood at the window, staring into the darkness. "Mr. McGrae?"

He turned and faced her. "Miss Lang," he responded with a polite tip of his head. "I be in need of yer forgiveness again."

"Sit." Hope's hands shook. She sat down where she'd been reading moments before.

Ian sat down and leaned forward.

"Miss Lang, I had words with yer brother today and I must confess I have held a secret that ye should be aware of."

She studied his face as Ian paused, looking at her with those sapphire eyes. She forced herself to focus. "If you must tell me, please continue."

"I must because I am as guilty as ye in wanting to break our betrothal. I came to America not to marry ye, but to break the bond and pay me father's debt. Yer sending the letter was an answer to me prayers. And yet I felt hurt and rejected. I am a very foolish man. I turned me anger to ye rather than accept me own guilt and shame for breaking me father's agreement. I know I am not the kind of a man ye would want to marry but I am wondering if we could be friends."

Hope swallowed and felt relieved. Tears welled in her eyes. What could she say? "It seems to me both of us reacted poorly to our parents' arrangement."

Ian sat back in the chair. "Aye."

"Why did you decide to come to America, to buy property?"

Ian smiled. "I had the funds and more to start a new life once I didn't have to pay me father's debt. I liked what I'd heard about the area, and there seemed to be a market for sheep, according to Mr. Leonardy, the butcher."

Hope chuckled. "I know who Mr. Leonardy is."

"Aye, that ye must." Ian's smile faded. "I don't know why I was so hard on ye. You're a remarkable woman."

Hope's stomach fluttered at his words. His brilliant blue eyes sparkled even in the dull lamplight as he smiled at her. "I like your smile," she blurted out.

Now he was grinning. "Aye, me mum thought she should have named me Fane, because it means happy."

"What does Ian mean?"

"It's like the name John, meaning God is gracious. I took a bit of ribbing over the years because it is mainly a Scottish name now. But me mum liked the sound of it, so I was named Ian Patrick McGrae."

"Patrick is a good, strong name." Hope relaxed. It was good to enjoy each other's company this way. It felt comfortable and friendly.

"Aye, it was me grandfather's name. Being the third son, all me father's names had been taken." Ian chuckled. "Fortunately, I wasn't the last son, like me brother Padraig Erinin McGrae, who also bears some of our grandfather's names."

"Padraig? What's that mean?"

"Nobly born. A fine name if ye are meant to be a saint, which Pad is not."

Hope laughed.

"'Tis good to see ye laugh, Miss Lang. But I must be gettin' on. Conall and Tara will be wonderin' what I'm about."

"Thank you for coming, Mr. McGrae."

Ian stood up and stepped toward the doorway, then turned back toward her. "If it be no imposition, or improper, would ye dine with me, Miss Lang?"

Hope's pulse quickened. "I don't know how long Grace will be needing me."

He nodded.

He looked so disappointed that Hope jumped up and

came to his side. She reached out, grabbed his arm and whispered, "Ian."

His eyes implored hers.

"I do forgive you. I need time, and Grace does need me."

Ian smiled. "Ye are right, it isn't the right time. Ye are a good woman, Miss Lang. I wish I hadn't been such a fool. Good night."

"And I, too," she whispered after he exited through the front door.

Chapter 5

Ian spent the next month clearing the land, repairing the barn and fences and making everything ready for his sheep to come from Ireland. They would be a part of his breeding stock. In the meantime, he'd sought out local stock, traveling hundreds of miles via steamboat along the St. Johns River. At the end of the month he had fifty head of sheep that seemed to be enjoying their new home. Conall and Tara were doing their job and doing it well. Tara was slowing down a bit with her pups about to be born, so Ian relied on Conall to do most of the work.

"Come, Tara." She waddled up beside him. "Good girl." He patted her head and gave her a drink. She lapped it up quickly. "Rest, Mum. Your time is soon."

Ian couldn't wait to see how the young pups would look. His mind traveled back to Grace Arman. She was still with child and encouraged to do nothing around the inn.

Hope continued to work at the inn but was no longer living there. He'd seen her on more than one occasion when he'd been invited to the Langs' for dinner by Gabe. Oddly, he felt at home with Hope and her family.

She continued to impress him. He'd learned that she was an asset to her father's investment business. She helped analyze the income and expenses. She put numbers together quickly in her mind. He often wondered why her father hadn't hired her to work at his office but understood she was now being paid a consulting fee for bringing in clients. It was rare even in America to see a woman in business, and truthfully, she worked behind the scenes. But those who knew the family well knew Hope played an important role.

He got up from the porch and went inside. As for financial reports, he had some of his own book-work to do. He sat down at the table with his ledger in front of him. Even with the outright purchase of the land, Ian still had reserves.

A knock at his door drew his attention. "Come in, door's unlocked."

"Forgive me, Mr. McGrae, but I should not," came the muffled sound of Hope's voice through the closed door.

Ian jumped up and answered it. "Hope—Miss Lang! What a pleasure to see ye."

She bowed her head slightly, her soft red hair cascading down her shoulders. "Forgive my boldness, Mr. McGrae, but…" She paused.

Ian looked at her closely, and could see that something was wrong. "No imposition at all. How may I help ye?"

"I learned some information today that might affect you and your property. I don't know how to say this, but there is a claim against this land. Someone is claiming

Mr. Sanders was not the owner and did not have the right to sell it to you."

"A lawyer drew up our agreement. How could the land not have been his?"

"That's why it surprised me, as well. I was looking at the town records investigating something for my father when I stumbled upon the claim. It might have some validity."

Ian stepped onto the porch, brushing past her. He leaned against a post and gazed upon the rolling green pasture. After all the work, and the sheep he'd purchased, what was he going to do? "What do Mr. and Mrs. Sanders say about this?"

"I didn't speak with them. I came to you. I thought you should know."

"I appreciate ye letting me know this."

"I think you should speak with Mr. Sanders, ask if he has his original purchase agreements for the land, especially the surveyor reports. Then you and Mr. Sanders need to secure a lawyer to represent you and take the matter to court, if need be. My guess is that someone is lobbying a false claim but I can't be certain.

"At a cursory glance, the claim seems legitimate. However, I have concerns. For one thing, the claim that Mr. Sanders didn't have the right to sell the property to you seems odd since he and his wife have been living on this land for forty years."

Ian took in a deep pull of air. "Then we need to speak with Mr. and Mrs. Sanders straightaway. Will ye come with me so ye can share what ye have found?"

Hope nodded. She pulled back her hair into a soft bun.

"Ah, ye had yer hair down for me," Ian teased, surprising himself almost as much as he surprised her.

Pink infused her cheeks as she stammered, "No, I just didn't take the time to put it back up."

"The pink on yer cheeks goes well with the fire in yer hair." The poor woman could barely speak. Ian sobered. Maybe he had been inappropriate. This wasn't the time to tease her. "My apologies, Miss Lang. Let's go see if the Sanderses are home."

Ian petted Tara and told her to stay. He whistled at Conall and the dog came running. "Watch the sheep, boy. I'll be back." They headed up the pathway that led to the Sanders home. "Tell me, Hope, if ye had yer druthers, what would ye like to do in the future?"

"Honestly, I'd like to fashion clothes."

Ian stopped. "Really?"

"Yes. There are many things impractical about women's clothing, like bustles for example. Whoever designed them… well, I don't know what he was thinking. The fact that it became the fashion rage for so many years boggles my mind. I think a slim, trim skirt with just enough room to walk or run is more than a woman needs."

"Isn't that what most women wear around the house?"

"Yes, but I'm thinking in the business world. A woman should be free to move as easily as a man and yet still be feminine."

Ian couldn't argue with the part about 'being feminine,' and he didn't know this country well enough to know what the business world was like. "Ye might have a point there."

"Most people don't believe women will be working more outside the home. But I see changes happening since the war. The women who were left behind had to tend to their family needs, pay their bills when their husband's income was gone or never arrived to them from the field. It's brought about a confidence in women. Look at Grace and what she does at the inn."

"Yes, I can see yer point. But don't ye think a woman needs to be home to raise the children?"

"Of course. But for those seasons when there are no children I believe we can do so much more."

Ian found her ambition attractive. In fact, everything about her was attractive.

Hope pored over the paperwork that Mr. and Mrs. Sanders provided. They were stunned that someone would try to make a claim on their land. She scribbled down notes of plot numbers, dates of purchase, the original owner's name, moving through each document until she came to the bill of sale between the Sanderses and Ian. "Ah, I think I have found the problem," she said as she scanned the details.

William jumped up. "What is it?"

"Look here. In the original draft from the lawyer, the number is 607.86 for the plot of land. In the final draft the number is 608.76."

"All of this because of a typographical error?" Mable asked.

"Hopefully it is that simple. Here are my notes. Take these to your attorney and he should be able to fix the matter without much fuss. However," Hope cautioned, "it is still troubling that someone would use this to make such a claim against you."

Ian stood up and placed his hand on her shoulder. "Thank ye, Miss Lang. We would have missed that! In fact, we missed it back when we signed the paperwork."

"You're welcome. If there is anything I can do just let me know. I have a pretty good eye for details and I'm fairly good at researching documents."

Mable smiled. "I'd say you're more than competent, dear. Thank you again for all your help."

Hope nodded. "I better get going before the sun sets."

"Ian, you should escort this young lady home," William prodded. "It isn't right to have such a pretty young woman walking by herself."

Hope chuckled. "Thank you for the suggestion, Mr. Sanders, but I drove the carriage."

"Oh. Well, in that case you should be getting home before dark."

"Yes, sir. Good night, all."

"Good night."

Ian hustled over to the door before she reached it. "I'll walk ye to yer carriage."

"Thank you, Mr. McGrae."

Outside, a pink-and-purple ribbon was forming on the horizon as the sun settled in the west. Just then, a sharp howl rent the air and Ian bolted toward his house.

Hope ran after him. Something must have been happening with the dogs or the sheep. She lifted her skirt and pumped her legs harder, trying to keep up. Her heels sinking into the soil, she dug up the ground like a plow turning over the dirt for the first planting.

Tara lay moaning on the porch as Ian petted her head and her belly. The dog was panting hard and about to give birth. Suddenly and without explanation, Ian left Tara's side as Conall growled out in the field. He ran toward Conall, calling out to Hope to please stay with Tara.

She rubbed behind the ears of the beautiful dog, sliding her hand to her tummy. "Oh my, you have quite a litter in there." She could feel at least four if not six distinct puppies.

She heard Ian yell off in the distance, then whistle.

Tara whimpered. "I'm here, Tara. I'll help you through this."

Ian came back drenched in sweat, his face drawn, carrying Conall. Hope saw the blood on Ian's shirt. "What happened? Are you all right?"

"A bobcat was trying to get one of the sheep. Conall fought him off. How's Tara?"

"About to give birth."

Ian groaned. "Hope, I hate to ask this of ye again but would ye stay with the dogs? I want to round up the sheep."

"I'm fine. I'll clean up Conall."

"Ye can find some rags on the floor of me closet."

"I'll be fine. Go, take care of your sheep."

"Thank ye." Ian laid Conall on the porch. "Stay," he ordered. He grabbed his shepherd's crook and ran off.

"Let me see what that bad bobcat did to you, boy."

Conall looked up with one blue eye and one brown eye. "Shh, boy, I know how to clean a wound. Let me get the rags."

Just then the Sanderses came over, William carrying a shotgun. "What was all that commotion?"

"Oh dear, what happened?" Mable asked, looking down at Conall.

"Ian thinks he tangled with a bobcat."

"I'll gather thread and some needles," Mable said as she headed toward the house.

"Miss Lang, should I send word to your family?" William asked.

Hope let out a nervous chuckle. "No, it won't matter. They'll understand once I explain everything." *I hope.* "Tara is about to deliver her puppies and I'm about to get some rags to clean up Conall's wounds."

"Mable will help you when she gets back. Best to let

Tara do what's natural." William hoisted his shotgun over his shoulder and went into the field to help Ian.

Hope stepped into Ian's home and headed for the closet. She hadn't been in the house since the eve it had been built, when she and the ladies set up the furnishings and the curtains.

This was a private side of him she had not seen until now. Ian kept a tidy room, just as she would have expected. She pulled aside the curtain to the closet and found the rags Ian had mentioned. She knelt down and fingered through the various materials. Selecting the more absorbent cloths, she started to rip them into strips.

Hope went back to the porch to see Mable returning.

"He needs stitching?"

"Yes. Not too bad, though. He should do well if infection doesn't set in. You're a brave boy, Conall," Mable encouraged while petting behind his ears.

Hope had readied a bowl of warm water to wash the wound as well as the clean rags. "This is going to hurt a bit, boy." Mable sat by Conall's head and held him down. Hope rinsed the wound then put in a couple of stitches. Conall whimpered but laid still. Hope was again impressed by how well these dogs obeyed.

As she wrapped the wound with the strips of cloth, she heard the sound of bleating. "Looks like the sheep and men are coming in," Mable said. "I'll go open the gate to the pen."

Hope couldn't believe the size of Ian's flock. There was no way they would all fit in that one pen. "How many sheep does he have?"

"Fifty."

"I don't think they'll all fit," Hope said

"They will. They won't like it, but they will fit." Mable

smiled. "Same with cattle. You can round 'em up until they squawk at yah, but they'll fit."

She loved watching him work. He was firm but gentle with his sheep. His movements were easy and fluid, relaxed. He leaned down and slid his hand down the legs of one of the sheep. Hope closed her eyes as an unbidden thought of being in his arms overwhelmed her.

Ian looked over and saw Hope sitting between Conall and Tara on the porch, stroking them with her gentle touch. The puppies lay beside their mother. Ian smiled. Somehow the porch looked more inviting with Hope sitting there. He prodded the small flock into the enclosed pen. "Thank ye, Mable and William. I appreciate yer help."

"More than happy to lend a hand. Here's my shotgun. Use it if that bobcat comes back tonight."

Ian nodded and walked over to the porch. "How are they doing?"

"Tara seems to be comfortable now that she's a mum with six adorable pups. Conall is doing well. We cleansed his wound and put in a couple of stitches. Where'd you get all the sheep?"

Ian shrugged. "I've been traveling a bit, purchasing some here and there. I'm hoping the five coming from Ireland will be here next month. I'll be getting me ram then, as well."

"How large of a flock do you want?"

"I'm not certain. Me original goal was five hundred. But I don't want to stress the land too much and I'm not ready to hire a crew. If I can have three hundred after two years I'll be happy."

"That's a lot of sheep."

"It takes quite a few to make a profit. But I'll be content to make ends meet in me third year."

Hope nodded. "I'm impressed with your knowledge and goals."

"Sheep raising has been in me family for generations. I be carin' for sheep when I was a young fella of five. Perhaps before, but I remember when I was five." Ian suddenly jumped up. "Forgive me for waggin' me tongue. It is late, and ye will be ridin' home in the dark."

"If you will light the lanterns for me on the carriage, I'll be fine. I'd like to stay and help with Tara but it wouldn't be proper."

"Aye. I'll take care of the lanterns."

Ian hustled off to the carriage before he said or did something totally inappropriate. *I was such a fool, Lord. Hope is a remarkable woman. Any man would be proud to have her as his wife. Give her safe journeys tonight, Lord.*

Hope bent down and kissed each dog, whispered in their ears. For the first time in his life, he was jealous of his dogs.

"Good night, Mr. McGrae. I'll be back tomorrow to see how Tara and Conall are doing. Can I bring you anything? I can't see you leaving the ranch for a couple of days."

"Aye, that be true. I'll be needing some eggs and bread."

"I'll take care of it. You try and get some rest."

"Thank ye, Miss Lang."

"You're welcome." Ian watched as Hope went to her carriage.

How much better it would have been to have her by his side as his wife right now. Ian wagged his head then turned his attention on his dogs. "Come inside, there be a bit of a chill in the air tonight."

Conall whimpered but obeyed. Thankfully, he was walking all right. Ian lifted the linen with the pups and Tara followed behind, keeping her eyes on her pups. Ian looked down at his sweat- and bloodstained shirt. He poured some water into the basin and cleaned his hands and arms. Then he put his shirt in the water to soak out Conall's blood.

He was grateful the Lord had spared the dog. Florida seemed to have quite a variety of predators. As soon as the dogs were fit he'd recheck the fence. Bringing fifty sheep into the area must be like offering a fresh steak dinner to the bobcat. He rubbed his chin. He'd better consult with Jackson Hastings and William Sanders again about the threats to his livestock.

Ian went back out onto the porch, watched his sheep and sat long into the night. Thoughts of Hope danced in his head. She was remarkable, kind, loving… Was there any way he could court her after all that had happened?

Chapter 6

Hope stopped by Ian's every day for a week to help him with errands. Today Conall's stitches would be coming out. He had been subdued every visit, but Hope could tell the dog wanted to be out running about.

She liked the way Ian doted on his dogs. Would he be the same way with children? But why would she wonder about that?

Ian had been herding the sheep back and forth each day without his dogs while Conall was recovering and Tara was nursing. Tara had six adorable pups, four male and two female. Hope fell in love with all the pups but especially the runt of the litter, whom she named Clare. She sported two brown patches, one over each eye. The tip of her muzzle was white.

Hope placed Ian's supplies on the table and went to Tara's bed, where all six pups were actively nursing. "How are you doing, Tara?"

Tara opened her eye but didn't lift her head. Hope reached into her pocket and pulled out a piece of beef jerky she'd brought. "Here you go, girl, a special treat."

Tara took the treat but stayed in place for the sake of her puppies.

"And how are you, boy?" Hope asked Conall. She flicked her wrist—the signal Ian had shown her—and ordered, "Come."

Conall wagged his tail and ambled to her side. Hope looked at his healing wound. Ian had made and applied an ointment to keep the infection level down. "It's looking good, boy. Would you like me to take them out?"

Conall woofed.

Hope sat back. It was the first time the dog had ever barked in response to a question from her. "Do you understand me, boy?"

"No, he saw me."

Hope jumped up and spun around. Ian leaned against the doorjamb, displaying his joyous grin. "But he does trust ye."

"Mr. McGrae, you startled me."

"Aye, ye were quite attentive to me dogs. I came to take Conall to work the sheep for a little bit."

"Is he ready?"

"Absolutely. However, I'd be remiss if I didn't keep that wound covered for another couple of days."

Hope wiped her hands on the apron of her skirt. "You'll find the items you requested on the table. Also, I brought you some fresh biscuits from the inn."

"Thank ye. How is Mrs. Arman doing?"

"Quite well. The doctor said she could start doing a few more things around the house. Which is good because Grace isn't one to sit down for too long."

Ian smiled. "Aye, I understand. I don't know how to

thank ye for all the help ye have been to me." He looked down at his work boots.

Hope swallowed. She prayed he'd stay in the doorway. The desire to be in his arms grew with each passing day. She came by to help at times when she knew he wouldn't be at home.

He raised his head and focused on her. "Ye are a godsend, Miss Lang."

"It is a pleasure to help. Now I must be off. I have to take in the sheets and iron some items for the Armans before my day ends."

"Oh, ye should know the lawyer was able to fix the records. Even so, I was served a legal notice today. Me attorney said it was nothing and he would handle it."

"This really makes no sense at all. I can't believe the judge agreed to hear the case."

"It does baffle. But I will trust the Lord."

Hope smiled. "That is a good attitude."

"I have to or I would not sleep."

Ian paused and then took a step into the house, closing the gap between them to little more than three feet.

"Hope," he whispered. "Would ye dine with me once the dogs are fit to be on their own?"

Hope locked onto his penetrating gaze. Unable to face her own growing attraction, she closed her eyes. "I don't think I should."

He took another step closer. "Ye must know I care for ye. And if I'm not mistaken, ye care for me, too."

Hope struggled to hold back tears, then focused on Ian's luminous blue eyes. Her heart sank. "I'm sorry, I..."

Ian squared his shoulders and stood soldier straight. "I know." He reached out his hands. Tentatively, she placed her hands in his open palms. "Father," he prayed, "Hope and I are scared and confused as to whether or not we should pursue a relationship. We ask Ye to guide us and help us to know if this be Thy will and not our own. In Jesus's name, amen."

"Amen," she repeated, then opened her eyes and met his gaze. "Thank you." A calm washed over her.

"'Tis me pleasure, and I meant every word, Hope. I'm as confused as ye."

Hope chuckled. "We are quite a pair, you and I."

"Aye, that we are, me love, that we are."

Hope's eyes widened.

"Sorry, I meant it as a term of endearment, not as a proclamation of me love for ye."

Hope nodded, her heart pounding wildly in her chest. She certainly knew enough of her Irish heritage to understand the term of endearment. "I better go now."

He released her hands and stepped to the side. "God's blessings, Hope."

"And on you as well, Ian."

She left his place as if her feet were being licked by the fires of hell. Every part of her wanted to wrap him in her arms and kiss him. But they would need more to build a relationship than their physical attraction and romantic feelings for one another. A lot more. *Did he have to be so handsome, Lord? And why'd You give him such incredible eyes? They light his soul and reveal his heart. He's such a strong and direct person. You know how much I like that.*

Ian was falling in love with Hope. He knew it; she knew it. But he had to agree, it was too soon. Nearly two months had passed since his arrival in St. Augustine. He'd given up on her before he'd even met her. He'd never even wanted to get to know Hope Lang. He had decided sight unseen she wouldn't be what he wanted in a wife, but now with each passing day he saw new signs of how wonderful she would be as his wife. Then again, she was raised with wealth and prosperity. Perhaps she didn't see him as worthy?

"If I can't be patient and wait for her, I am not worthy, am I, boy?" He looked down at Conall. "Let's remove those stitches. Lie down."

Conall obeyed. Ian knelt down beside him and with the tip of his knife cut each stitch and gently pulled them out one at a time. "Good boy." Then he put some salve on Conall's wound and wrapped him up with the bandage Hope had purchased for him. "I've got to stop thinking about her, boy."

"About who?" Gabe stood in the doorway.

Ian groaned. "I need to remember to close doors."

"Wouldn't matter, you don't have windows yet. So, who do you need to stop thinking about?" Gabe teased.

"Doesn't matter, she's not available."

"Well, then, that is a problem." Gabe came in and sat himself down at the table. "I brought you some lunch and I wanted to speak with you about your investments."

"I don't have any investments."

"Which is why I wanted to speak with you." Gabe smiled.

Ian rubbed the back of his neck. "I take it this is what ye do for work?"

"Yes, I'm a financial advisor. You have a lot of money sitting in the bank. I can help you make that money work for you."

"I'm not a fancy man, Gabe. I'm a simple man. I invest in me work and I work with me hands."

"I'm not saying that's a bad thing. In fact, I think it is a good thing. Land and livestock are good investments." Gabe passed over one of the paper-wrapped sandwiches.

"Can we sit down? I'm not going to pressure you into buying or investing right now, mostly because I do not know your business. But it can't be too much different than the beef market. Buy low, sell high—it's that simple. However, there are many variables that a man must consider. Your pups for instance. I figure you'll be training them, but you won't be needing all six. Those can be sold to some of the cattle ranchers in the area. Everyone is amazed by your dogs."

"I raised, trained and sold dogs in Ireland. Mostly Irish sheepdogs. Truth is, ye could earn eighty pounds sterling back in Ireland for the sale of a well-trained hunting dog, but I sold sheepdogs for fifty pounds. At the current exchange rate that would equal two hundred and fifty dollars American, which I don't think a farmer would pay."

Gabe sat back in his seat. "You're probably right. What do you think they'd be worth here in Florida?"

"Don't know." Ian unwrapped his sandwich and took a bite. "I figured I would have to wait and see what kind of market would be available for me. There is a reason I took them with me everywhere I went." Ian winked.

Gabe laughed out loud. "Touché. So you don't need my advice after all."

"I didn't say that. But I may not be as lost as ye might think."

"Good, then I'd like to learn more and see if I can help advise you?"

Ian nodded. "I'd like that." *And maybe ye can clue me in about yer sister.*

They finished their lunches and Gabe headed back to the city. Later that evening Ian started working on his ledgers, replaying his conversations with Gabe and with Hope. As complicated as his relationship with Hope was, Ian didn't want it any other way. He'd been turning down some invitations to dinner with local families, suspecting they were nothing more than attempts to match him with their daughters.

He knew it wouldn't be fair to give any hopeful young ladies ideas because his heart was not free. Not with his feelings for Hope growing every time he met her.

He glanced at the figures. He still had plenty of money, and within six to seven months' time he'd have that litter trained and ready to sell. Life was looking profitable in America—perhaps not as profitable as back in Ireland, but profitable nonetheless.

Ian was in good spirits until early the next morning, when the sheriff banged on his front door. "Mr. McGrae, I have a summons for you," he announced.

Ian pulled the door open to find Sheriff Bower in full uniform, holding an official-looking envelope. "What kind of summons?"

"Can't say, it's sealed. I was ordered to deliver it for the courts."

Ian broke the seal and scanned the letter, his heart sinking as he read.

"What? This can't be! Why?" he said.

In that moment, all he wanted was to speak with Hope for clarity and her calming influence.

But he was on his own this time.

Hope finished cleaning the rooms, washed and hung the first batch of laundry and was cleaning up the morning service dishes when Grace came into the kitchen. "Good morning, Hope."

"How are you?"

"Fine. Actually, I'd love to run and jump but I can't do that just yet."

Hope laughed. "I'm glad you're feeling better."

"Tell me what's been happening. How are you and Ian getting along?"

Hope glanced to the ceiling then focused on Grace. She was a good friend and perhaps she could help her with these confusing emotions. "That could take a while."

"Then I'm all ears. Let's have some tea and make ourselves comfortable." Grace went over to the stove and put the kettle on.

Hope finished washing the last pot. "First, tell me, are you still expecting?"

"The doctor believes I was carrying twins. I might have lost one, but the other baby still seems to be growing."

Hope didn't know what to say. She'd never heard of such a thing. She couldn't imagine what Grace was feeling or thinking.

"It's rare, but does happen from time to time. In another month we'll know for certain. We're waiting until we know for sure if I'll be able to carry the baby before telling Richard's parents, or the rest of the community."

"Twins? Oh my, and you can still carry one of the babies?"

"Yes. But as I said, it is rare. I don't know what I would have done without you, or my mother. She's been wonderful. Of course, this will be her first grandchild. Father is beside himself. It's amazing the change in him. He respects Richard now and can't apologize enough for his behavior in trying to force me to marry men I had no interest in." Grace took a sip of her tea and looked over the rim at Hope. "So…have you kissed Ian yet?"

"No!" Hope protested a little too loudly. "Sorry, no."

Grace laughed. "But you've thought about it."

Hope groaned. "Well, yes. Have you looked at him? He's gorgeous. His smile can brighten an entire room.

And his eyes… Goodness, a girl could get lost in those sparkling blue eyes."

Hope sobered and hung her head. "Ian has asked me to dine with him twice, but I said no. Even though I wanted to say yes."

Grace patted her hand. "What are you afraid of?"

"I've never had feelings like this before, Grace. I didn't expect to be scared by such strong emotions. And, well, I still feel the blow to my pride and confidence because of what happened with my job."

"Oh, Hope. Sometimes you just have to take a chance. And I think your heart is telling you to take a chance on Ian."

Chapter 7

Ian paced back and forth in the front room at the lawyer's office.

"Mr. McGrae!" The door to the inner office swung open and Ben Greeley came out, right hand extended. "How can I help you?"

Ian handed him the summons. Ben's eyebrows rose. "This doesn't make any sense. I know this judge fairly well. Let me look into it and I'll send a message over to your place."

"Thank ye, Mr. Greeley."

"I've been looking into the clerical error you found on the bill of sale and we can't seem to track down where it happened. But I've petitioned the court to make the proper changes. The new paperwork should be ready in a day or two."

"Again, thank ye, Mr. Greeley. I've been tied down to the ranch for the past week because Conall was attacked by a bobcat and Tara just gave birth."

Ben smiled. "You wouldn't be interested in selling one of those pups, would you? My children would love a puppy and yours are so obedient."

Ian chuckled. "We might be able to barter on that. I sold them for fifty pounds sterling in Ireland, that's two hundred and fifty American."

Ben's eyes widened and he whistled. "That's a bit much for a childhood pet."

"I understand." Ian smiled. "I also won't sell them to anyone who doesn't have a large enough property for them to run. They are working dogs and need to exercise, or they would not be happy."

"Ah, we have a fairly good-size courtyard but probably not large enough for your dogs."

"What do I do about this?" Ian pointed to the summons.

"Nothing at the moment. I'm going to speak with the judge personally and see if I can get the case dropped before a court hearing."

"I will wait to hear from ye. Good day, Mr. Greeley."

"Good day, Mr. McGrae."

Ian left the attorney's office and headed for the Seaside Inn. He wanted to check on the Armans and see how they were doing. Not to mention the possibility of running into Hope. He came up to the kitchen door and knocked. Inside he saw Grace and Hope in an embrace. Hope wiped her eyes. She'd been crying. He suddenly wanted to wrap her in his arms, offer her some protection against whatever was bothering her. She glanced over at him and gave a halfhearted smile.

Ian's pulse raced. Awareness solidified in the core of his being as he realized he'd been the topic of her discomfort. He smiled back at Hope, then pulled his attention toward Grace. "Hi, I came to see how ye are feeling?"

"Better, thank you. And how is Conall?"

"Fine. Hope's talent with the needle helped and he is his old self again."

"Hope's been telling me all about Tara's puppies. I think you'll find there will be a long list of folks who might like one."

Ian chuckled. "Not once they hear the price I used to get for them in Ireland."

"Oh?" Grace asked.

He briefed Grace and Hope on the cost and exchange rate, and they had the same response as others. There was no sense letting folks think he would be giving his puppies away at no cost. It would be like giving away a steer. His dogs were income and investments.

Hope's smile faded. "I guess I shouldn't get too attached to Clare, then."

Ian smiled. "I'm afraid not, darlin'. Being female, she can produce more puppies once she's old enough." As much as he'd love to give Clare to Hope as a gift of appreciation, it simply was not good business.

"They are exceptional dogs," Grace admitted with a smile and grabbed her cup of tea. Hope did the same.

Feeling very much the intruder, Ian asked, "Where might I find Mr. Arman?"

"In the barn."

"Thank ye. Good day, Miss Lang, Mrs. Arman. I'll keep praying for ye and the little one."

Grace's eyes widened. "You know?"

"Sorry," Hope apologized. "Ian came by the first night and I told him then."

"Oh, sorry. We're not announcing until we know for certain the baby is all right."

"Mum's the word then, Mrs. Arman." Ian winked and

slipped out of the kitchen. He headed to the barn and found Richard working. "Richard?" Ian called.

"Ian, good to see you."

"How are ye?"

"Fair. I'm concerned for Grace."

Ian lowered his voice. "I know about the little one."

Richard smiled. "And I'm concerned about the baby. The doc thinks she may have been having twins and lost one."

"Aye, I'm sorry to hear that. I've seen it with me dogs and livestock," Ian said. "I'll keep ye in me prayers."

Richard nodded.

"I wanted to thank ye for the recommendation of Ben Greeley. He's been quite helpful."

"He's a good man."

"I can't stay long. I left Mrs. Sanders with the dogs and I can't leave Conall to oversee the sheep yet. But since I was in the city I thought I should come and check on ye and the missus."

"Thank you, I appreciate it. I'm looking forward to some of your lamb. When do you think you'll be ready to trim your flock?"

"It'll be a while. These new sheep are not as hardy as I'd like. I'll soon get them fattened up and strong. Me ram should be coming soon and we'll see how the first breeding season goes."

"Fair enough. But know that I'll be one of your first customers."

Ian smiled. "I'm certain we can work something out."

"Ian, one more thing. I'm aware of Hope breaking your betrothal. And I'm aware of how much she's been helping you. Please be careful and treat her right."

Ian shrugged. "I've asked her to accompany me to

dinner and she's turned me down twice. I don't see a re-lationship developing between us."

"I'm sorry to hear that. Thank you for stopping by," Richard said as he extended his hand.

Ian made it home by midafternoon. He watched the puppies nursing and squirming around Tara. She was a good mother and patient with her pups. Their eyes were not open yet, but would be soon.

His thoughts turned to Conall, and he found him watching the sheep from the porch of the house. "Good boy, Conall. Ye want to run, don't ye, boy?"

Conall jumped up. Ian flicked his wrist and Conall jumped off the porch and hit the ground at a full run. He couldn't blame the dog—he'd been stuck in the house for his recovery. Ian glanced up at the blue sky. No hint of rain. But he'd learned that rain storms come up without much notice in Florida.

As he watched Conall run and frolic, his mind drifted back to Hope and the tears in her eyes. He hated the idea of causing her pain in any way, for any reason. His stom-ach twisted a notch. He should have submitted to his par-ents' agreement with the Langs. Then again, would she have been happy marrying a lowly shepherd?

Ian closed his eyes and tried to give his life, his fu-ture, back to God. The "if onlys" were going to drive him crazy. The Langs' blue two-story Victorian house with white-and-blue trim came into his mind, speaking volumes about Mr. Lang's success and social standing.

He scanned his little cottage. There was no compari-son. He couldn't imagine Hope being happy here.

Hope couldn't believe Ian had showed up at the Sea-side when he did. She'd never been so embarrassed, and she could tell he knew she'd been crying about him. She could see it in his eyes, the compassion, the confusion, then the recognition of what she and Grace had been talking about.

Hope groaned. She pulled the sheet out of the wringer and hung it on the line. She definitely liked office work a hundred times better than doing laundry. But she would do it because Grace needed her help. And she would do it without complaint. Laundry was nothing compared to taking care of the chamber pots. Hope groaned again.

"Sorry, Lord. I know I shouldn't be complaining. I'm where I need to be." Hope glanced around the yard to make certain she wasn't being overheard. "Father, direct Ian and me about the kind of relationship we should have. We are attracted to each other, but I want more, so much more than simple attraction."

Hope finished hanging the laundry then set out for her own house. Her household chores were being neglected, and while the sheets and towels were drying at the Seaside she could get some of her chores at home done.

"Afternoon, Mother," Hope said as she entered the kitchen through the back door. "What smells so good?" Hope sniffed the air. "Don't tell me, corned beef and cabbage?"

"Aye, that it is, dear. I made some extra for Mr. Mc-Grae. Are ye going to see him this evening?"

"No, ma'am. He came to town today. I'll stop by tomorrow." Hope lifted the lid of the pot and sniffed.

"Are ye done at the inn?"

"I have the laundry to finish. Everything is drying on the lines but I'll need to fold and iron some of the items before I can call it a day."

"Aye, I know the process."

"Mum!" Gabe hollered as he came in through the back

door and reached into the cookie jar. "Are you cooking corned beef and cabbage?"

"Aye, I made a large pot so we can share with Mr. Mc-Grae. Are ye going to see him tonight?"

Gabe sat down and munched on a cookie. "Wasn't planning on it but I'd be happy to bring him some. I was speaking with him about investments and— I don't know why, but I was surprised at how good he is with finances. Do you know what his dogs sold for in Ireland?"

Hope laughed. "You can fill Mum in. I have some chores I need to get done before I return to the Seaside." Hope left the kitchen and headed up to her room. As curious as she was about Gabe and Ian's conversations, she had a limited amount of time to get her work done.

She straightened, cleaned and dusted the room within an hour then sat down at her desk and wrote in her journal. The pages before her had provided a place of confidentiality where she freely expressed the guilt and shame of dishonoring her parents by going behind their backs and writing that letter to Ian. Her pen hovered over the page as she wondered if her parents had known better right from the start, especially given what she'd come to feel for Ian after all. "Why did I resist my parents and their plans, Lord?"

She glanced at the clock, closed her journal and headed back to the inn. She continued this pattern over and over again for the next week—work, chores, journal and back to work.

Tonight Ian McGrae was coming to dinner again. She'd managed to leave him notes and pick up his purchases without seeing him for more than a moment. It was better that way.

A gentle knock at her door caused her to stop writing in her journal. She blew on the wet ink. "Who is it?"

"Ye Mum."

"Come in."

The door opened slowly. "Are ye all right, darlin'?"

"Fine, Mum. What can I do for you?"

"Nothing." Sally Lang sat down on the bed facing her daughter. "Are ye hiding? You spend all yer time at the inn or the house. Ye have not ventured out in a very long time."

Hope faced her mother. "I'm not trying to avoid anyone."

"I am concerned with yer fears." Her mother smiled. "Ye have not had much contact with Mr. McGrae. Are ye afraid of him?"

"Not of him, of me. I can't trust my emotions. One minute I'm angry and upset with him, the next I'm tempted to show more love and compassion than a sister in Christ would show to another."

Sally reached out and took Hope's hands. "I shall pray ye find peace around Mr. McGrae, and I shall not invite him for dinner again until ye are at peace."

"No, Mum. I don't mind Mr. McGrae coming to dinner. He's a fascinating man."

Her mother squeezed her hands. "I know, darlin'. Come, help me make some Key lime pie for dessert."

Hope smiled. Key lime was her favorite. And perhaps helping to prepare the meal for Ian might be the action she needed to take to calm herself down. After all, it was just dinner with the family. There was no he and she. She was probably thinking far too much about it. She didn't like these feelings of insecurity. She'd never had them before she'd been fired by Hamilton Scott for doing her job.

Focus on Key lime pie, she reminded herself, not Ian McGrae and her insecurities.

Ian walked past the white picket fence and up the stairs to the Langs' front door. He was nervous.

He raised his hand to knock. Of course, Hope could be working at the inn tonight. He tapped as the door opened. Gabe stood there with his reddish-brown hair neatly combed back, appearing every inch the business-man in his fancy suit. "Ian, it is good to see you, my friend."

Ian smiled. "And it be good to see ye again, too. How are ye?"

"Good, good. I've made a profit for some of my clients today, so it is a very good day."

"Congratulations." Ian gave a slight nod in Gabe's direction. "Ye work hard for it."

"Not hard enough. I haven't convinced you."

Ian chuckled as Drake Lang stepped into the foyer. "Let the poor man in, Gabriel."

Gabe stepped back and Ian stepped into the now familiar front room and hallway of the Langs' home. Drake greeted him with a hearty handshake. "How ye doin', son?"

"Fine, thank ye." Ian shifted. The differences between this home and his own… "Me sheep are doing better and Conall is quite happy that he's able to run and work the sheep. I've repaired the fence, although I believe the bob-cat can probably jump it."

"You're probably right. But the fence will discourage them some." Drake motioned toward the sitting parlor. "Come and sit. Can I get ye something to drink?"

"Some of Mrs. Lang's limeade would be nice."

"I'll see if she has some." Drake left and Gabe sat down.

Ian tried not to scan the house and look for Hope.

Gabe grinned. "She's in the kitchen helping Mum."

Just as Ian was about to insist that he wasn't concerned with Hope's whereabouts, a scream from the kitchen pierced the air. Ian and Gabe jumped up and ran to help, Ian's heart pounding with worry that something had happened to Hope.

Chapter 8

"Gabe, get the wagon ready!" her father ordered.

Hope tried not to think of the pain. Her body was shaking. Her father had her wrapped in his arms, holding her up. Mother dampened yet another hand towel. "I'm sorry," she kept saying, over and over.

"It was an accident, Mum," Hope groaned.

"What happened?" Gabe asked as he and Ian ran into the kitchen. Gabe took one look at his sister's bleeding arm and his eyes opened wide. "I'll have the carriage ready in a minute."

"What can I do?" Ian asked.

Hope looked down at her arm. Her mother wrapped another towel over the wound with shaky hands. "Hold this." Her mother demonstrated. "Hold it tight."

Ian came up beside her and held the cloth down over the wound. Tears fell down her face. She didn't want to cry, but the pain... Was the injury worse than a simple cut? It had to be. She'd never experienced pain like this before. Her mother had been chopping a coconut while Hope held it in place for her. The knife slipped. Her mind was a blur. The throbbing pain clouded everything.

Gabe hollered from outside, "Carriage is ready."

"Can ye walk, child?" her father asked.

"I'll carry her," Ian offered. Worry and concern etched his handsome face.

Her father gave Ian a sharp retort simply with his eye-piercing gaze. Hope had seen that gaze on many occasions growing up. It was pretty obvious Ian understood it, as well.

"Forgive me," Ian mumbled.

"Ian, ye hold the bandage. I'll help Hope down to the carriage. And I'll be driving the carriage to Dr. Peck's office." Father used his firm don't-bother-to-challenge-me voice.

Ian nodded. "Yes, sir."

Hope wanted to giggle but pain and good manners kept her from such an outburst. Her father escorted her to the door. Ian, on her other side, held the towel tightly around the wound. She could feel his breath near her ear.

"I'll be prayin'," he whispered.

Those simple words meant so much. The pain seemed to subside a bit. She glanced down. She could see her blood on Ian's fingers as he held down the towel.

Mother followed. With each step her mother sniffled. "I'll be fine, Mum."

"I'm so sorry, darling, so, so very sorry."

Her father stopped and turned to his wife. "Sally, it was an accident. Nothing a few stitches won't take care of."

"I'll meet you at the doctor's office," Sally said, her

voice strained. Hope wished they had a larger carriage instead of the Jenny Lind that only sat two comfortably.

"I'll clean up the kitchen for ye," Ian offered.

Hope wished he would be coming.

Gabe helped her up into the carriage. Her father took his place and grabbed the reins. "Dr. Peck's, Sally."

Gabe released her. Hope clamped down on the blood-soaked towel—too hard, and she cried out.

"Yah!" her father yelled, and snapped the reins. The horse bolted forward.

Tears fell. There was no holding them back. She turned and saw her mother removing her apron, then receiving a tender embrace from Ian. His compassion warmed her heart.

Gabe and Mrs. Lang left shortly after, following the carriage to Dr. Peck's office. Ian stayed behind and cleaned the counter, placed the food back in the pot and covered it with the lid. He washed the dirty dishes and scanned the kitchen again for anything out of place. Hope's wound was deep. She might have severed an artery, the way the blood spurted out.

"Ian," Gabe called out. His heavy footfalls echoed through the hall. "Are you still here?"

"In the kitchen. How is she?"

"Doc said he had to do surgery to stitch some of the inner tissue together. Which means he'll immobilize the arm for a while to help it heal."

"I understand. I cleaned up and the supper is back in the pot. If ye think you'll be gone longer we should heat up the food to keep it fresh."

"Father and mother are consoling one another. I felt kind of awkward and out of place. Mum is beside herself, sayin' it was her fault."

"It be an accident. It isn't anyone's fault," Ian added.

"Exactly. I'll go back in an hour, but I thought I'd come by and let you know what was happening. Are you hungry?"

Ian looked at the full pot of roast beef and vegetables. "Aye, that I am. I suppose I shouldn't be but…" Ian tapped his stomach.

"I am, too. Come on, let's eat. Then I'll return to Dr. Peck's. We can't let Mum's good cooking go to waste."

"Aye, that we cannot."

They ate and spoke about nothing in particular, about everything…except Hope. Ian could tell that Gabe was concerned for his sister. "Does the doctor feel she'll heal well?"

Gabe nodded. "She's just had so many tough situations put on her in the past few months with work and the betrayal she felt from Hamilton Scott. Then you arrive and, well, I know my sister. She cares for you, and based on the way you've been looking after her today, you seem to care for her, as well. But this whole betrothal situation is getting in the way. Hope's always had a confidence that was unshakable. Now…" Gabe paused. "Now, it appears that she doesn't trust herself, her judgments or anything. I understand her desire to help Grace out at the inn. But she has far more to offer than simply changing bed linens and cooking breakfast."

"Ye sister is a rare jewel. She'll regain her footing again."

"Is that what you want, Ian? Do you want her to regain her footing again? And possibly find another man?"

"I am not bound to yer sister any longer. I have no rights."

"Don't you?" Gabe leaned in toward him and narrowed his gaze. "I may not have found the woman for me yet, but I can see you have regrets concerning Hope. Life is too precious. Look what happened this evening. Don't waste any time."

Ian stood up. He needed distance from Gabe. He rubbed the back of his neck. "I should be going." Ian started toward the door.

"Ian, I'm sorry. I'm just worried about Hope."

Ian relaxed his shoulders. Gabe was, as he said, worried for his sister, and it was more than the injury she had suffered tonight. It was the injury to her heart and the changes she'd been making in her life, about many of which he was still clueless. But it wasn't his place to ask. "And I understand that, Gabe. Tell yer family they are in me prayers. Good night, Gabe."

Ian wanted to check on Hope but, as he'd just pointed out to Gabe, he had no rights regarding Hope Lang or her family.

He headed home in the dark, alone, thinking on all the "if onlys" he'd missed by breaking off his betrothal to Hope.

The next morning Ian went straight to the Langs' place to seek out Hope and check on her. He stepped up to the two-story Victorian and knocked on the door. Mrs. Lang answered it, wiping her hands on a towel. "Mr. McGrae, it is good to see ye. How are ye? We are grateful for your help yesterday."

"I'm fine. I came to see how yer daughter is doing."

"She's going to be just fine." Mrs. Lang's puffy eyes told the story of a sleepless night of worry.

"I am glad to hear that. Is there anything I can do?"

"That is a generous offer, Mr. McGrae, but there is nothing. She's upstairs in her room resting."

Ian wanted to see her, but knew it was not the right

thing to do. He nodded. "Thank ye again for letting me know. Have a grand day, Mrs. Lang."

A slight smile creased her lips. "I shall try, Mr. Mc-Grae."

Ian reached out and placed his hand on her shoulder. "It was not yer fault, Mrs. Lang. It was an accident."

Sally Lang shook her head. "It was a horror to behold. My hands tremble just picking up the knife."

"You'll feel better once ye know she's healed and doing well," he encouraged. He stepped back. "Would ye be so kind as to tell Miss Lang that I came to check on her?"

"I will. Thank ye again, Mr. McGrae, for everything ye have done. God's blessings, sir."

Ian nodded and stepped back. He had begun to think of the Langs as family, but now he felt a distance from them, a separation. It was probably for the best. He stepped out on the street and turned to see Hope standing at the window. He waved. The flash of a white bandage caught his eye. *Heal her, Lord.*

As he worked his way back to his ranch he realized he *should* keep his distance. Hope didn't need a man of meager wealth and possessions. She needed a man who could give her all the desires of her heart. He thought back on the furnishings in the Langs' home. Each piece was finely crafted. Yes, Hope Lang grew up in comfort, more comfort than a shepherd's wife would have.

The weight of his realization settled over him as he walked. It was the last visit he would pay to the Langs' home. Hope didn't need to be reminded of the past. She needed to heal. Not only from the wound on her arm but from the wound in her heart, whatever that might be.

Resolved in his decision, he devoted himself to his ranch, his flock and his dogs for the next week. But he missed her. Just about every waking moment, his thoughts drifted toward Hope.

Ian sat down on his front step and scanned the field. Tara lay on a mat Ian had fashioned for her. The six puppies were all drinking to their hearts' content. Clare, the runt of the litter, finished first. Her wide tummy full, she waddled over toward the edge of the mat. Ian chuckled and scooped her up. "Ye are a cute one, Clare." Hope had named her and it seemed to fit. She had blue eyes, each with a patch over them. "How ye doing, girl?" he asked, holding her up for inspection.

Her tail wagged back and forth, brushing his hands. He brought the puppy bundle to his face and kissed her.

"Hi, stranger." Ian jumped.

Hope apologized. "I'm sorry. I didn't mean to startle you." But she'd been mesmerized by the sight of the sweet scene before her. Ian was strict with his dogs, but tender, too.

"How are ye? How's the arm?"

"Dr. Peck said it is healing well." She held up her arm for inspection.

"What actually happened that night?"

"I was holding a coconut for Mother when the knife slipped and sliced my arm."

"How bad was the injury?"

"The knife cut deep. The big concern is nerve damage. However, I can wiggle my fingers and still have feeling in each one." She scanned the ranch. "You've been working hard."

"Aye, it keeps a man honest." Ian smiled.

"The puppies look good." Hope was struggling for conversation. She'd been aching to see him since the accident, to thank him for what he'd done for her, but somehow the words wouldn't come. She felt shy around him, unable to forget the feeling of being in his arms.

"Tara is a good mother. Clare is doing well. She's still the smallest, but she be strong and healthy." Ian paused then took a step toward her. "Hope, I don't want to cause ye pain but is it wise for ye and me to spend time together?"

Hope stepped back then turned her back to Ian. She closed her eyes. What had she been thinking? "I don't know. Perhaps you are right. I'm sorry for…" Ian stepped right beside her. She wanted to turn and be wrapped in his embrace as Clare had been moments before, nuzzled and kissed by Ian. "I'm sorry, I shouldn't have come."

Ian nodded.

She gazed into his eyes. Her pulse quickened. "I wanted to thank you for helping me after the accident."

"It was me pleasure, Hope."

"It has been a difficult few months since I was… I'm sorry, I can't."

"I be here if ye would like to discuss it."

"Not now, Ian. I can't."

"It can't be worse than I am imagining."

Hope looked away from Ian's penetrating eyes. She couldn't tell him what happened when she was working for Hamilton Scott. She still didn't understand it herself. How could she explain it when she didn't know?

Ian reached out and placed his forefinger under her chin and lifted it until their eyes met. "I am concerned about ye not being confident in who God made ye to be. Ye are an astute woman. Ye calculate numbers and figures in yer head faster than any other person I know. And yet ye spend yer time changing bedsheets."

Hope turned away. Did she want this much honesty between them? "You don't understand."

Ian took her by the shoulders and turned her around, his eyes brighter than she'd ever seen them before. He stepped closer and cupped her face in his hands.

"Then explain it to me," he said. He pulled her to him and she stepped into his embrace as his lips captured her own. His kiss was like nothing she'd ever experienced before. There was a depth to it that calmed her even as her heart began to race.

He stepped back. "I'm sorry, I should not have done that."

Hope blinked her eyes open. She started to shake.

"I'm sorry, Hope. I should not have…"

She reached out and caressed his face. "Nonsense."

He wrapped her in his arms for a few long moments then gently pulled away a bit. "Hope, can ye honestly see yerself living in this cabin?"

Hope looked at the quaint wooden structure then back at Ian. She placed her hands on his chest and stepped back. "For a time, I suppose I could."

"Aye, and that be just one of the problems between us."

Hope cocked her head. "Are you saying that because I would want a bigger home one day that it would be a problem between us?"

"Aye. I am a simple man, with simple needs."

"And I am…" She motioned for him to finish the sentence.

"Ye need more than a simple home."

"I understand now. I am not the kind of wife you want." She felt the heat rise up her neck and face. "You want one who would be content living in this one-room house with babies at her feet, cooking your meals without a thought or concern about one day having more."

"No, it's not that. I'm not sayin' this proper like. I like ye, Hope, very much but…"

"I understand." She spun around and headed for the door.

What had she ever done to say to him that she wouldn't be content with a humble home? A good, sound home, albeit a bit small. No family could be expected to live in a small place like that with children forever, could they? "I shall see you around, Mr. McGrae."

She wanted to turn back, but her pride kept her moving forward. She'd thought they had a chance of developing a real relationship. In the end, there wasn't any ground to build upon. He viewed her as a rich socialite and nothing more, even though she'd been spending her time cleaning chamber pots at the Seaside Inn.

It didn't matter. She had other things to do, other plans. Loving Ian McGrae was not a part of those plans, and that was fine. At least that's what she tried to tell herself as she walked away.

Chapter 9

Ian sighed as he watched Hope walk out of his life. He'd been right to bring up the possible problem in the beginning. She needed to know his concerns and obviously he'd been right. She would not be content living in his single-room house.

Tara lifted her head and let out a whimper. She, too, would miss Hope's kindness and affection. Ian groaned. He shouldn't have kissed her. He knew kissing Hope would stir up all kinds of emotions but he never expected a kiss to be so powerful. It was more than their lips meeting; their hearts seemed to blend, as well.

How could that be?

"I'm sorry, girl. I'm afraid Miss Lang will not be a part of our lives." That's twice he'd ruined a chance at happiness with a woman who could be a mate of incredible worth. The Proverbs 31 scripture of an ideal wife had a verse about that, if he recalled. He went into the house and pulled out his Bible, opening to the thirty-first Proverb. "Who can find a virtuous woman? For her price is far above rubies."

"I found her, Lord," he said aloud. "But I don't have the rubies."

He closed his Bible and headed for the back pasture to bring his sheep in. It was time to stop regretting the decisions he should have made. Even if he had honored the betrothal she would never have been happy in his meager cottage. She was a precious jewel worthy of someone with more.

Then the first part of the verse hit him again: "a virtuous woman." How virtuous could she be? Granted, he didn't know exactly what happened but his mind went to her being put in a compromising situation. What else could it be? But then again, she wasn't the type… He argued with himself the entire time he walked out to the pasture.

"Who am I to judge Hope, Lord?"

He saw her at a distance in church the next Sunday but declined to speak to her. What could he say? He turned to leave and Gabriel came up beside him. "Haven't seen you around much."

"I've been busy."

Gabe nodded.

Out of the corner of his eye, Ian saw a man approach Hope. She stiffened. He reached out for her. She pulled away. Ian marched toward Hope. He needed to protect her.

Gabe grabbed Ian's arm and stopped him. "I'll handle it."

Gabe spun around and headed over toward Hope and the stranger. Before Gabe got to them the man sidled away.

Ian's back stiffened. Ian glanced at the retreating individual and noticed he was wearing gentlemen's clothing. His gaze turned back to Hope. Gabe had his arm around her and was leading her out of the sanctuary. He glanced back at the gentleman and took a step forward. He might not be from the same social class but manners and proper respect toward a woman, any woman, especially Hope, demanded a reprimand.

"Ian, it's good to see you." Richard Arman came over and shook his hand. "How are you? How's that flock coming?"

"They are healthier. Me ram and the five sheep from me father's herd should be arriving in the next few days."

"Depending on the winds and rains."

"Precisely. How is yer wife?"

"Better. She still isn't ready to come to church and sit on the hard pews for the entire service but the doctor says she's doing well and we'll be able to announce the good news to folks soon." Richard beamed. Ian didn't know if he'd ever seen a man happier at the prospect of becoming a father.

"How's the issue regarding your property going?"

"Slower than a snail crossing a path of salt. Mr. Greeley is surprised at the pace. The judge saw that it was a false claim and rescinded his order but another claim was filed with another judge a couple of days later. It is all very peculiar."

"It is strange. I've heard of border disputes before, but most of those have been squared away and both parties agreed to the new survey. But this, there is something odd about it."

"Ben agrees. He's working to try and find the person responsible for the claims and it seems he's finding other errors." Ian leaned in closer. "He believes someone be changing the titles and claims. Thankfully, the Sanderses still had their original paperwork."

"I will continue to pray for you and the Sanderses. This must be weighing on them."

"They seem to be taking it in stride. They know they owned the land and have their deeds all in order. I wish I were as trusting as they are."

"There is something to be said about getting older and knowing the Good Lord will make things right even if you have to struggle for a while."

"Aye, they have that peace."

"And you, my friend, do not, do you?"

"I've been trying to trust the Lord but I keep running back to me own judgments from time to time."

Richard tapped him on the back. "Don't we all, my friend, don't we all. It's been good catching up with you."

"Give Grace me love and prayers."

"Thank you, Ian. Good day."

"Good day." Ian watched as Richard Arman headed off toward the Seaside Inn. Richard was a lucky man to have such a loving wife at his side, one who worked just as hard as he did. Ian paused his thoughts. Hope could be that kind of a wife, too. The voice in his head flashed through all the times he'd seen her working hard for her friend.

Did I misjudge again, Lord?

Hope dressed for the Dia de Muertos, the Latin holiday known as the Day of the Dead. Folks who were not from a Hispanic background were surprised and a bit bewildered by the event. She smiled at the thought. In true tradition, it focused on remembering friends and family who had passed away. Where it went a little too far for Hope's taste was in bringing food to the graves or building private altars to their ancestors. However, she loved the festive atmosphere, the parades, the music and the celebration.

And today, Hope needed some cheer. Hamilton Scott approaching her in church was a bit more than she'd expected. It had been nearly four months since he'd fired her for no reason. Well, there was a reason. But he didn't want to hear the truth about the careless documentation of his employees. Mr. Scott wanted her to come back to work for him, no apology, no admission of any wrongdoing on his part. And she was to simply accept his offer as if nothing had happened?

Hope would not submit herself to that kind of treatment again. Because she was a woman, he saw her as expendable, and she knew, given the right circumstances, he would fire her again with no cause. What bothered her most was his approaching her in church, hinting that if she would simply apologize…

But worse than her encounter with Hamilton Scott was seeing Ian and knowing he thought her unworthy or unwilling to love him as he was. The ever-present knot in her stomach twisted again. Especially in light of the kiss they had shared.

Hope sighed. She looked in the full-length mirror at her dress. It was bright and colorful, giving the impression of happiness. She would not let anyone know her heart and her feelings of unworthiness. At one time, she would have thought it impossible that she would be so insecure, but there was no denying it now. She'd been judged by Hamilton Scott to be unworthy. And she'd been judged by Ian to be unworthy of his life and life choices. She couldn't work for her father in the investment company because people wouldn't accept a woman in that business. Besides, he already had a secretary who'd been working for them.

"What am I good for, Lord?"

She sat down in the reclining chair in her room and opened her Bible to the familiar verses from the thirty-first Proverb. "'She seeketh wool, and flax, and worketh willingly with her hands.' I don't work with wool or flax but I do quilt and like working with fabric and designing dresses." Even Grace had asked her if she wanted to be a dressmaker. She nibbled her lower lip. "Should I, Lord? Should I strike out on my own?"

She read further. "She considereth a field, and buyeth it." She had been earning some money and her father had started to pay her for her time going over some of the business proposals.

Hope got up and walked over to her desk. She started a list of the various steps one would need to take to start a dressmaker's business. She would drive through St. Augustine and count how many dressmakers lived and worked in the city. Knowing the competition was one of the first requirements for assessing whether or not a business would be sound.

For the first time in months, she felt better, like she had a plan. She continued mapping out the necessary steps and what she would need to investigate until her mother called her. "Are you coming?" Sally Lang asked from behind the closed door.

"Sorry, Mum. I'll be right down." Hope left her paperwork on her desk. She had a new direction for her life, a new purpose. She might not have a husband or any prospects at the moment, but she was encouraged.

She realized she'd forgotten who she was. God didn't make mistakes, and being a woman didn't make her any less adept in the business world. She could, and with God's grace she would.

She opened her bedroom door and hurried down the stairs, where the rest of the family was waiting for her. The bandage was still on but she didn't care. Today she would choose to have fun, enjoy life and not put herself down. Yes, she'd made mistakes, but who hadn't?

Her mother smiled as she approached. "Ye are beautiful, Hope."

"Thank you, Mum."

Her mother wrapped her arm around Hope's waist and whispered in her ear. "I'm glad you're feeling better, Hope. I trust ye have forgiven yourself."

Hope nodded. Had she? Yes, she had, and it felt wonderful to be free from the events of the past. It was time to look forward.

The next day Hope began in earnest to research the various dressmakers in St. Augustine, find out who owned a storefront and who worked from their home. By the end of the day she had gathered enough information to start analyzing whether or not it would be a profitable business. And if she were to start such a business, would she hire employees? How big did she want this business to grow? Or did she prefer to keep it small, enough for a bit of income… No, that wouldn't be good enough. She would need to eventually pay for her needs, to rent or own her own home, to completely provide for herself.

Would she design a line of clothing that she would prefer to wear, or a line that the social elite would prefer to wear, or both? Personally, she'd rather design clothes she'd like to wear, but from the few shops she'd entered earlier that day, she could see that making fancy gowns for the genteel ladies of society was a large part of the business.

She worked until she was called to dinner.

"Good evening, Father." She kissed him on the cheek and sat down in her seat.

"Good evening, daughter." He winked. The two of them had a running gag of being formal with each other for a moment at the table.

Gabe shook his head. Mother came in from the kitchen carrying the serving dish with roast beef, potatoes, carrots and onions with brown gravy. Gabe took the platter from his mother and placed it in the center of the table. "Thank ye, son."

"You're welcome, Mother." Gabe wiggled his eyebrows at Hope, making her laugh.

"What has brought ye cheer, Hope? It is good to see but I am curious," her father asked.

"I'm working on something. Give me a couple of days and I will share it with you. I'd like your input but I'd like to work out the details first."

Drake smiled and nodded. He reached out his hands and the family followed suit, each taking the hand next to them. With her left she was connected to her father. With her right she was connected to her mother, and Gabe sat across from her with the same connection. Her father led them in prayer, then they began the harmony of taking food items and passing the bowls and platters around.

Gabe opened the conversation, extolling his business prowess for the day. Hope listened. Her father plied him with questions, most of which Gabe had the answers to. Mother seldom said much when it came to business but when she did, it was always a well-thought-out comment.

"I've been speaking with Ian to learn about his business. This is beef country—I'm a little leery of just how much mutton and lamb can be brought into this market. However he did speak with several of the butchers in town and George Leonardy let him know that he never has enough for his customers."

Hope was curious to hear news about Ian but she fought the urge to ask any questions. She did not want to appear anxious or overly interested in Ian McGrae, the man who kissed her, then broke her heart.

"Don't forget specialized markets, son. A man can do quite well providing something different."

"I for one am looking forward to having more lamb on our tables." Mother spoke up. "Of course, your father and I grew up eating our fair share of it."

Specialized markets… Should she be considering her style of clothing as a specialized market? She knew some women on the frontier were making their skirts like pants so they could sit on a horse with the same ease as a man.

"What about the wool? Does he have a plan for that?" Hope asked.

"Yes. Apparently they shear the sheep at the early part of the summer then the animal has a good coat before the winter months."

Gabe cocked his head but didn't ask her any questions. He, more than most, probably knew that she and Ian were not suited for one another. Although she wished it could be different. She remembered the feel of his lips on hers. Hope looked down at her plate and closed her eyes. She would not think about that kiss again, especially not in front of her parents and brother.

"Mother, do you know of anyone who cards and spins wool in St. Augustine?" Hope asked.

"A few of the older ladies do. However, most sheep ranchers send their wool to manufacturing plants."

"I'll mention that to Ian. Thank you, Mum. By the

way, dinner is wonderful this evening." Gabe accented his words with the lift of his fork.

A round of praise went out thanking mother for her culinary skills. Hope's mind went over the process of shearing sheep to processing the wool, spinning it into threads, then making fabric... No, that wasn't for her. She preferred buying fabric already made.

Perhaps Ian was right. Perhaps she wasn't cut out to live as a shepherd's wife.

Hope closed her eyes and concentrated on who she was created to be rather than what others thought she should be. She would not slip into the mire of depression again. It didn't suit her, and if it were possible to stop oneself from going down that road, she would choose to.

A knock at the door stopped everyone. Father got up to answer it. "Mr. Lang..." Hope didn't recognize the voice but she did recognize the tone. Someone was in need or in trouble.

Chapter 10

Ian scanned the dock, looking for the right ship. Word had come that his sheep and ram were in port. He turned and looked down the street toward the Seaside Inn. He wondered if Hope was there this morning, helping Grace. He couldn't stop thinking about her being in his arms.

He shook off the thoughts as he approached the ship. He could see and hear the sheep bleating in their pen on the dock. A smile creased his lips. They were finally here.

He greeted the first mate and signed for his stock. He'd brought fresh water and oats, not knowing what his animals had been fed on board.

"Conall," Ian called. The dog stood at attention. Conall would help him walk the sheep back to the ranch. Ian hoped he'd made the right choice to walk them back and not transport them in a wagon. The animals would be in need of some exercise after the long voyage.

"They weren't a troublesome lot," the first mate said

with a smile. "Your father provided well for their care on board."

"Thank ye." Ian signed the paperwork and opened the pen door. "Stay, boy," Ian ordered. There was no sense making the sheep walk around the pen. He checked each of their legs and hooves. Satisfied, he opened the gate and encouraged them to walk toward Harbor Street. As the sheep exited the pen, Ian whistled, giving Conall the command to walk the sheep down the dock and toward the road.

Between Ian and Conall the sheep obeyed. They continued on until he reached the halfway point to his ranch. There he told Conall to rest. The sheep stopped moving and grazed on the green grass in front of them. His ram was a bit more cautious and surveyed the area for a moment before he grazed.

Jackson Hastings pulled up with his wagon. "Hi, Ian, these the sheep you been waiting on?"

"Yes, sir."

Jackson climbed down from his rig and examined the stock. "Fine-looking ram."

"Thank ye. Me father was very generous in giving him to me."

"Five ewes and a ram are a very generous gift. As a man who's raised livestock for most of my years, I know good stock. Can I give you and the sheep a lift to your ranch?"

Ian glanced at the sheep. They were tired. "That be right kind of ye. I should have brought me wagon."

"Glad to lend a hand." Fifteen minutes later the sheep were bleating in the back of the wagon. Conall sat up front with Jackson Hastings and Ian. "They don't know a good thing when they find it," Jackson said.

Ian chuckled. "That be true enough."

"How's the house working out for you?"

"Very well."

"You might consider building an addition after your stock is doing well, perhaps in the winter."

"House is fine for now."

"I suppose for a single man that would be true but… well, it isn't my place to say…"

"What?"

"I thought you were looking to get married one day. My wife and I started with a small house but we planned on building it larger and with a second floor once the children started coming."

Ian felt his cheeks redden. "If I find a wife, yes, I would need to build an addition."

Jackson smiled. "I don't mean to pry but weren't you and Miss Lang…?"

"Our betrothal was ended by mutual agreement when I arrived." Ian wasn't about to tell his personal business to a stranger, although Jackson was obviously close to the Langs if he knew about the betrothal. More importantly he didn't want to stain Hope's reputation in the community.

"Ah, I understand. She's a fine woman, though."

"Aye, that she is," Ian acknowledged. They arrived at the driveway to his property. "Ye can let us off here. The sheep will need to walk off their concerns about riding in the wagon."

Jackson chuckled. "They are a loud bunch."

Ian and Jackson made quick work of getting the sheep off the wagon and onto the road. Ian whistled and gave Conall the signal to bring the sheep down the lane. He turned back to Jackson and extended his hand. "Thank ye again."

"You're welcome. Come by the house sometime, perhaps a Sunday dinner. I'll check with the missus and let you know."

"That is most kind."

Ian stood there for a moment as he watched Jackson climb back up on his wagon and pick up the leather reins. Jackson turned and waved. Ian lifted a hand in reply. Ian paused. *How many people know about our betrothal?*

Hope sat at a small tea table with Sandra Allen, whose husband owned the local mercantile. A few strands of her ash-blond hair tumbled down the sides of her cheeks. Sandra kept her hair back with a rose-colored ribbon. They were enjoying a warm cup of tea, chatting about her husband's business, when a man carrying a bushel barrel of pumpkins came in. "Excuse me." Sandra went to the counter. "Looks like a mighty fine batch, Mr. Middleton."

"Thank you. I've got three more bushels in the wagon. Would you like any of those?"

"I think we can sell a second bushel."

"Thank you." Mr. Middleton placed the basket on the floor and hustled outside to retrieve another bushel.

Hope's mind raced over all Sandra had to think about in order to be prosperous in her business. For instance, items that could spoil could constitute a loss. Hope was glad she was going to be dealing in fabric. Hope thought she and Sandra could work out a deal where Hope would not have to pay the full retail prices since she would be purchasing the entire lot. After Sandra finished with Mr. Middleton she came back and sat down with Hope. "Where were we?"

"I'm looking into starting my own dressmaking shop." Hope went on to explain her desire to work with Sandra.

"I'll have to speak with my husband, but if you'll take

care of all the paperwork, and we simply have to be the receivers of the fabric, that sounds like a fair deal. When are you hoping to begin?"

"I'm still looking into storefronts, but I'm also considering working from my home until I build up a client list."

"Count me in. I'm in need of a dress that doesn't get in the way of hauling items up and down from the shelves, and that won't knock items off the display tables. I like that business outfit you made a while back for yourself. It was sharp looking and didn't come with excessive layers. So what would be the cost of one of your dresses?"

"I'll have to get back to you on the cost. I'm still analyzing the figures. I don't want to jump in and start a business without looking at it thoroughly."

"You always did have a head for numbers." Sandra leaned in a bit closer. "And business, like me," she whispered and winked.

Hope chuckled. "We don't have many dressmakers with shops in St. Augustine and there could be a good reason for that. One is that we are a major port so the latest fashions from New York, London and Paris are available at all times. Then there are our northern visitors who come for a season and then return. They come with trunks full of clothing."

Sandra leaned back. "You have a point there. Like I said, I'd love a skirt that didn't have the excess fabric but I don't want to be too modern. I'm not certain my customers could handle that."

"I understand. Let me take your measurements and I'll draw up a design or two."

Sandra beamed. "Could you make the skirt separate so I can change blouses if they get dirty with all the dust that comes off those shelves?"

"Anything you want."

Sandra went to retrieve her tape measure. Hope took her measurements and wrote them down in her notebook where she kept all her notes concerning this venture.

The door jangled as a new customer walked in. Hope looked up. Sunlight glinted off the chestnut hair of Ian McGrae, who paused in the doorway, his blue eyes sparkling. "Miss Lang, a pleasure to see ye."

"And you, Mr. McGrae." Hope knew she should leave but her feet didn't want to obey. Instead she sat back down at the table and poured herself another cup of tea.

"May I join ye?" Ian stood with his hat crunched in his hands.

Hope cleared her throat. "Sure."

"Thank ye," he said, pulling up a chair. "Me ram and ewes arrived earlier today."

"When will the breeding begin?"

"Soon." Ian cleared his throat and leaned in closer. "I feel terrible about the other day."

"Mr. McGrae, I'm afraid we are a bit like oil and water." Hope looked down at her lap. "We don't mix well."

Ian sat back. "Perhaps ye are right."

Sandra marched over with a bolt of fabric in her arm. "What do you think of... Oh, forgive me, Mr. McGrae. What can I help you with?"

"I'm in need of some red ochre and vegetable oil."

"Sure, I'll see what I have." Sandra handed the bolt of fabric to Hope.

Hope fingered the cotton fabric with a painted design of pink rose petals on a sea of blue-gray. It would make a beautiful skirt and vest for Sandra. She'd even put in a pocket like Grace had shown her when working as a laundress.

"Ye sew? Of course, ye sew. I saw ye at the house-raising party."

Hope stood up, counted to three and calmed herself. *How is it he can be so oblivious to how much his words hurt?* "Mr. McGrae, if you'll excuse me I have some errands to run. Would you please let Mrs. Allen know that the material would be perfect and that I'll see her in a couple of days?"

Ian stood and grabbed her arm before she could flee. "I'm sorry. I can't seem to say the right words with ye." Tears filled her vibrant green eyes. His gut twisted. "I'm so sorry, Hope," he whispered. He wanted to wrap her in his arms, to push all the distance between them away.

"You are forgiven, Mr. McGrae." She pulled away.

"I want more," he whispered.

She froze for a moment, and then continued out the door.

Had she heard him? Ian drew in a deep breath and sat back down at the small tea table. He'd never had much need for a fancy table. The teacups were finely made porcelain. He lifted a cup. It was English Derby porcelain, some of the best. He placed the teacup back in its saucer. These were the items that Hope Lang was used to in her life. These were the very items he could not provide for a wife. He closed his eyes and tried to remind himself that he was not the kind of man Hope Lang would need. She was meant for the finer things in life.

And yet, he couldn't seem to stop himself from pursuing her.

"Mr. McGrae," Mrs. Allen called from the counter. "I have the items you requested. Where's Miss Lang?"

Ian slid the cherrywood chair back and walked to the

counter. "Miss Lang said the fabric ye picked out would be perfect."

"Good, thank you for telling me. I take it you know Miss Lang?"

"Yes, her family helped with the building of me house."

"Ah yes, I heard about that. The Langs are good people. They're from Ireland, too. Did your families know one another?"

"Me parents are friends with Mr. and Mrs. Lang. But the Langs have not been back to Ireland for many years."

Sandra added up the cost and he handed her the money. "Pleasure doin' business with you, Mr. McGrae."

"Same here, Mrs. Allen. God bless ye."

"And you, sir."

Ian grabbed his items in the sack Mrs. Allen provided. "Forgive me for saying so," she said. "But Miss Lang is a good woman."

Ian smiled. "Yes, I know she is." He placed his hat upon his head and exited the building. He didn't need to be reminded about the kind of woman Hope was. He'd seen with his own eyes. He knew the warmth of her embrace, her kiss...

He caught a glimpse of Hope rounding the corner a couple of blocks down. Perhaps he should apologize again. He started toward her. *No.* He'd apologized. Clearly he just needed to stay away from her because it would be best for both of them.

He swung around in the opposite direction and headed home. He had a lot of work ahead of him and he couldn't be distracted with the beguiling features of Hope Lang.

Chapter 11

Hope ignored Ian's insulting comments about her social standing and calmed herself before entering the city clerk's office.

There were two locations in particular she was curious about. One was owned by a business corporation. The other had been in the family for many years but the grandchildren were planning on selling it. Of the two, the building on the second lot needed more work but it also provided a second level where she could live. She didn't have a huge desire to move out of her family home but if she purchased the property she could rent the upstairs and help pay the mortgage off faster. Did she have the equity to do so? In truth, she didn't. But her father did. Did she want to go into business with her father?

Hope worried her lower lip. Her musings were interrupted by a conversation loud enough for others to hear.

"I'm tellin' ya, H.W., you're askin' for trouble. You

can't pull this off. The judge has already asked for proof."

Hope's ears perked up. She scanned the office but saw no one. There were several smaller offices and storage spaces out of view of the public area. She glanced back down at the ledger she had open before her.

"But the guy said he's got proof."

"Have ya seen it?"

"No, but he says…"

"Hey, look, it's your life. But I wouldn't mess with it. I'm just sayin', it don't seem right. Where'd you meet this guy anyway?"

"Six months back. He's in and out of town on business all the time."

Hope tried to pull her focus back to the paperwork in front of her. The more she thought about it, the more practical it seemed to start her business from home. That meant no overhead…but also not much room, either.

Hope closed the ledgers. "Thank you," she called out to the Billy Newman, the assistant clerk who was still in the back room talking with H.W., whoever he was.

On her way home, she couldn't help but wonder what the two men were referring to. Naturally, her mind shifted to Ian and his land troubles, although that was being taken care of by his attorney. Then again, this H.W. seemed to be trying to cut corners, perhaps even skirt the law. Hope shook off the conversation. It wasn't her place to deal with the issue, nor did she know what the two men were actually referring to. *Stop trying to come up with another reason to see Ian. He's made it clear that you aren't the kind of woman he wants as a shepherd's wife.*

At home she found her mother in the kitchen canning some pumpkin and making watermelon-rind pickles. The watermelon would be a refreshing treat after walking around the dusty streets of St. Augustine. "Hello, Mum. You've been busy."

"That I have, darlin', that I have. Come, sit and tell me what has you running to and fro. You're done working at the inn, aren't ye?"

"Yes. Grace is healthy enough to work now. I'm still going to lend her a hand on the weekends when they have a lot of guests. But she's past the worst and out of danger. She and Richard are sending a letter to his family and they're looking into hiring a chambermaid."

"They will be so pleased to hear about the baby." Her mother grabbed a towel and wiped her hands. Then she set two oyster dishes on the table and filled them with chunks of watermelon. "I do love watermelon."

"Me, too." Hope forked a cool chunk of the sweet red cubes.

"You still haven't told me what you've been up to the past few days."

"Oh, well, I'm looking into the possibility of starting my own dressmaking business. I'm thinking I have to start small and work from the house but I don't know that I have the room to spread out enough. I certainly can't cover the dining room table with fabric every day."

Sally Lang laughed and said, "Ye are right about that."

"I can't afford to rent space in town without first building some equity. I'm between that proverbial rock and a hard place."

Her mother put down her fork. "Hope, ye do know yer father might be willing to invest…"

"I know, Mum. I'm trying to do this on my own. I'm not above asking father for help but I'd like to have all the facts and figures in front of me. I did however gain a client today. Sandra Allen would like me to design a dress similar to that business outfit I designed and made last year."

Her mother chuckled. "It was practical, but it sure wasn't the latest style."

Hope grinned. "That's why I'm leaning toward the design aspect of the dressmaking. Many women I know want practical clothing. Perhaps I can hire some gals to do the sewing."

"My, my, ye do have big dreams." Sally put her arm around Hope. "Now. Tell me what's happening between ye and Ian."

Ian scanned the barn to determine how much grain and hay he'd need for the winter months. Next season he would plant some hay and grasses for his livestock but this year he'd be dependent on what they could eat from the land and what limited grain he could provide for them. Sheep, unlike cattle, would eat the grasses right down to the soil, which meant a longer time for the grasses to return.

He walked up to the pen he'd put the ram in. "How ye doing, boy?" The ram ignored him and continued munching on the fresh hay. "Looks like ye are adjustin'."

Ian glanced up at the pound of red ochre and vegetable oil he'd purchased at the mercantile, then remembered his encounter with Hope. Was she right that they were like oil and water?

He grabbed the gallon of oil and marched over to the house. Inside he found an empty mason jar that had contained canned vegetables. He poured some water in the bottom of the jar, then stopped and went back to the barn. He opened the red ochre and dipped his finger into it. Again, he went to the cottage, placed his finger in the water, instantly turning the water red. Ian smiled. It reminded him of Hope and her red hair. Then he poured the same amount of oil into the jar. Placing the lid on tight, he shook it. Bubbles of water and oil mingled. Then he put the jar on the table. As it settled, the oil and water separated. Ian sighed. Perhaps she was right.

Tara was lying on the floor with her six puppies crawling around her. Some were nursing, others were playing. He pulled Clare up from the lot. "How ye doin', girl?" She yawned, her pink tongue stretching out and curling back into her mouth. Ian cradled the pup close to his chest. "Ye are a cutie." He couldn't help but wonder if Clare was taking a special place in his heart because she was Hope's favorite. *Hope. She just doesn't understand the real problem with our different social classes.* He'd love if that wasn't an issue between them, but he knew better. He'd seen it more than once back home in Ireland. It just didn't work. After a few minutes of snuggling and petting the pup he returned her to her mother.

He glanced back at the jar. Most of the bubbles were gone. The red water sat on the bottom and the oil lay on the top. He took the jar and shook it again, harder this time, even though he knew the two would never completely blend.

Ian put the jar back on the table. He would use it as a reminder not to get lost in unrealistic hopes and dreams. Hope was right—they would never blend.

So why had he been unable to stop himself from saying "I want more"?

"Mum, I don't know what to say. There isn't a relationship developing between us. At least not a pleasant one." Hope stood up and started to pace. "We seem to bring out the worst in each other. We can't share more than a couple of sentences without the other saying something to offend, even when trying to be careful." Hope sat down again.

Her mother paused for a moment. Her gaze seemed to penetrate deep into Hope's soul. Hope glanced away. Her mother grabbed her hand. "Ye have forgiven yourself. I can tell."

Hope grabbed her mother's hand with the other. The warmth and strength she felt in her mother's grasp surprised her for a moment. "Yes, I've forgiven myself. I didn't fail Hamilton Scott's business. And while it was wrong for me to go behind your backs in writing to Ian to cancel our betrothal, I have forgiven myself for that, as well."

Her mother nodded and smiled. "And yet, there is something between you two."

The color in Hope's cheeks brightened when she realized how much her mother knew. "He's behaving in such a confusing manner. One moment he's…" Hope trailed off, not ready to tell her mother about the kiss.

Her mother squeezed her hand. "Come, let's go to the parlor. There's something I'd like to share with you."

Hope allowed her mother to take her by the hand and bring her to the front parlor. They sat together on the small settee, with its high, curved back and arms, which gave the impression of an intimate embrace. Many deeply personal conversations between them had been had on this couch.

"When my mum informed me that I was to marry your father, I was quite upset, in much the same way that ye were."

Hope narrowed her gaze.

"Your father and I both felt the obligation to go through with the marriage but it took a month after we were married before we truly started to open up with one another. Getting to know your father, allowing him to be the man he was meant to be, allowed me to open me eyes. I would read the passage from 1 Corinthians 13 over and over again, and I would see how each day I was not loving my husband as I should."

"But you didn't know him."

"And that be my point. I don't know for certain if Ian is the man for ye. I do know that there is a spark of interest between ye. He cares about ye, even if he can't express it. I've watched him look at ye when he thinks no one else is looking. He cares deeply how ye feel about him, too."

Hope shook her head. "I don't know, Mum."

"No, ye do not. Tell me, darlin', when was the last time ye prayed for your spouse?"

Hope sat back. When was the last time? When she was sixteen and was told about her betrothal? For years she had prayed for him, not knowing who he was but trusting him to God's care and protection. "I hate to admit it, Mum, but it has been many years."

Sally tapped Hope's knee. "Then that be the place to start. If Ian is to be your spouse then everything will fall into place. If he is not…well, then ye will just have to wait a bit longer."

"When did you and Father start to love one another?"

A slow smile grew. "It was that day I mentioned, a month into our marriage. We carried on in a horrible fight. Ugly words were said, not worth repeatin'. But as we let our tempers calm we started to open up with one another. We discovered we had a lot in common. And yer father isn't hard on the eyes." Her mother winked.

Hope chuckled. "I love you, Mum. Thank you."

"Ye are welcome, darlin'. Now go to your room and freshen up a bit. Your father is takin' us out to dinner tonight."

Hope stood and gave her mother a heartfelt hug. She made it up to her room, each step a bit harder to climb. Had it really been five years since she'd prayed for her would-be spouse? Would she have written to Ian if she had continued to pray? Would she know whether or not Ian was meant to be her spouse if she'd been praying for him all these years?

Dear Lord, how can I have been so stubborn and self-absorbed?

Chapter 12

Ian fingered the hair from his face and rubbed his eyes. He hadn't slept well and there was only one reason for that—it had something to do with a certain redhead who stirred his emotions. What was worse, he was feeling guilty over his refusal to have her be his wife. Betrothal or not, he came to America determined not to have anything to do with her, and yet she'd been nothing but kind to him.

His evening devotionals had brought him to 1 Peter 4:8. "And above all things have fervent charity among yourselves: for charity shall cover the multitude of sins."

And Ian knew he had not been charitable to Hope. He'd been rude. That had him flipping over to the thirteenth chapter in 1 Corinthians. His charity—or rather his lack thereof—stood out like the St. Augustine Lighthouse, which was slipping into the ocean, inch by inch. His charity was drifting out to sea when it came to Hope

Lang. He needed to mend fences once again, and to stop doing things like kissing her, and then telling her she wasn't right for him, and then telling her he wanted more.

Somehow he'd need to control his emotions and be clear, and not…not what? Assume? Was he assuming too much when it came to Hope? Ian scanned his humble cabin. "*Could* she ever be comfortable here?"

Ian turned to see if Gabe would suddenly appear as he had before. Thankfully, Gabe was not there. Ian got up, fed the dogs and prepared his breakfast. He looked forward to the day when he would have an icebox and could keep milk. Instead he crunched on dried granola and drank down some lukewarm tea. He drafted a note of apology, put Conall out to patrol the land and checked on the recent additions to his flock from Ireland.

He found the ram in just about the same location munching on the hay. The ewes were huddled together in their pen. He wondered if they were already impregnated. The captain said he'd had them all in the same pen on board the ship, which could mean his first lambs would be born a month before the others. Ian smiled. "Good, that will give me a practice run to make certain everything is prepared for the birthings."

After his morning chores he cleaned up and headed toward the city. He wanted to speak with Hope, or at least make arrangements to speak. His fingers traced the folded paper he'd put in his pants pocket. At the very least she'd have his written apology.

He walked up to the Langs' home. It stood proud with its two stories and upper and lower porches. White scroll-work glistened in the sun, accenting the clapboards. It was a beautiful house. Ian took in a deep breath and let it out slowly, then marched up to the front door and knocked.

A moment later Mr. Lang came to the door. "Mr. Mc-Grae, how can I help ye?"

"I'd like to speak with Miss Lang."

Drake Lang, dressed in a three-piece business suit with a gold chain that draped from the button on his vest to the small pocket for his watch, leaned back on his heels. The man's attire spoke volumes of the difference in net worth between himself and Ian. "I'm afraid she is not here this morning. She's out scouting some possible locations to rent."

"Rent, sir?" Ian couldn't believe Hope would move out of her parents' home.

"She's undertaking her own business. It's really quite a remarkable plan she's put together. She and I were discussing it last night. Can I give her a message for ye?"

"Yes, please." Ian handed Hope's father the note. Mr. Lang took it and slid it into his pants pocket. "Thank ye, sir."

Drake Lang nodded. "Have a good day, son."

A tumble of footsteps came down the stairs behind Drake, drawing Ian's attention. "Ian, what are you doing here so early?" Gabe asked.

"I had a message for yer sister."

"I've been going over your figures. Do you have a few minutes?"

Ian nodded, pulled off his hat and stepped inside the house.

"Let's discuss it in the dining room. I haven't eaten yet and mother doesn't like it when I hold up her plans."

"I heard that," Sally Lang's voice floated back from the kitchen.

"How's yer sister's arm healing?"

"Fine, fine. She can move all her fingers. There will be a scar, but not too bad."

"I still have nightmares seeing her arm open like that."

Gabe shuddered. "Don't get me started. Have a seat. Have you eaten?"

"Yes." Ian looked over the array of pancakes, syrups, eggs and bacon, and his stomach grumbled.

Gabe laughed. "Mum, can we have another plate for Ian?"

"Coming right up."

"Thank ye, Mrs. Lang. I haven't eaten like this since I left the Seaside."

Ian sat down. Gabe sat in the chair beside him, and Drake took his place at the head of the table. "I've been going over the figures you gave me concerning the amount of grain your sheep will need," Gabe began. "I know your plan is to grow what you need next year, but I was thinking about the needs for this year, and was wondering if you might be interested in trading your ram's services for some hay."

"I'm not sure. From what I saw of the sheep in the area, I'm not sure I'd want to put the ram at risk. Keeping me stock healthy is very important to me and there is still so much I don't know about this land, the insects, the dangers to the sheep…everything. I'd rather wait for another year, then I might consider it, once I know the land better."

Gabe nodded. He forked some pancakes and sausage onto his plate and passed the platters to Ian. "I understand."

"Ye should speak with Jackson Hastings," Drake interjected from behind his newspaper. "He'll be able to give you sound advice about the insects and such. I know his business is cattle but he's known for keeping his herd healthy."

Ian agreed, mumbling around a mouthful of pancake.

The front door opened and closed. A woman's heels clicked on the hardwood floor.

"Mum, I'm…" Hope's words trailed off as she came into the dining room and saw Ian sitting there with her father and brother.

Unfortunately, she looked none too pleased about it.

Hope stood with her mouth agape. She closed it as her father turned toward her, putting his newspaper down on the table. "Mr. McGrae came to see you this morning and your brother tagged him with some business questions." Her father reached into his pocket and pulled out a folded piece of paper. "He gave me this note for you."

Ian stood up, wiping his mouth with the linen napkin. "May I speak with ye, Miss Lang?" He took the note from Mr. Lang, then looked back and forth between her brother and father. "In private?"

Her father looked over the rim of his glasses.

"I only have a couple of minutes. I forgot my notes and came back to…" Hope stopped herself. It was so easy to speak with Ian. He'd made it clear—and yet he was here. With a note. "Sure, in the parlor. I'll be there in a moment."

Hope headed toward the kitchen and turned to see Ian walk into the parlor. She entered the kitchen, closed her eyes and counted to ten. Her mother came up beside her and placed a loving hand on her shoulder. "Shoo! Go put the man out of his misery."

With a nod, Hope spun around and went to the parlor. Ian stood at the window overlooking the front yard. "What would you like to speak with me about, Mr. McGrae?"

He turned and smiled. She kept her expression neutral. She wouldn't allow herself to be pulled in by that smile, not again. Not now.

"I'm afraid I've come to apologize once again. It seems I've not treated ye with Christian charity. I had a long night with the Lord and He made me examine meself, again. I have no excuse. I don't know why…" His words trailed off. He slipped the note into his pocket.

"Ian," she whispered and stepped a bit closer. "I, too, have been in error. I was rude to you at the mercantile."

Ian shook his head. "We be quite a pair, ye and me."

"Like water and oil," she quipped.

"I tried that."

"What?"

"I mixed water and oil. If ye shake it real hard tiny bubbles appear and the two seem to mix. But when the liquid settles the oil and water separate. Slowly at first, but in the end, they become two separate liquids." Ian paused and walked back to the window. "Yer father said ye were looking for property to rent for a business?"

"Yes, I'm exploring the possibility of opening my own dressmaking business."

"Did ye make yer dresses?"

"Most of them. I'm not a fan of some of the styles that come from France and England. Of course, some of them are far too thick and layered for Florida heat."

"Me mum never had the luxury of wearing high fashion. Simple dresses and skirts for her and me sisters."

"How many brothers and sisters do you have?"

"There be five boys and three girls in me family. I'm number five. I have a brother and two sisters younger than me."

Hope motioned for him to take a seat. "I really can't stay long but I need to share something—something my mother and the Lord helped me to realize last night. It seems since I learned of our betrothal I stopped praying for my spouse. I had been praying for him since I was twelve and mother first spoke to me of such matters. In any event, I believe if I had continued to pray for my spouse I might not have written the letter."

Ian sat back. "I don't believe I ever prayed for me spouse. Of course, I've known about me betrothal since I was a lad." He played with the hat in his hands then looked in her eyes. "Interesting concept."

Hope chuckled. "My parents were betrothed in an arrangement similar to ours."

"Gabe told me," Ian admitted.

Just how close had Gabe and Ian become? she wondered. "Mum said she and Father had to get to know one another before they started to love one another."

Ian reached out and took her hand. "Hope—"

"I know what you said before, and I took offense at it. You judged me before getting to know me."

"Aye, I am guilty. But look at yer home, the furnishings ye grew up with."

Hope smiled. "And do you remember what you said when you challenged me about living a simple life in that cottage?"

Ian cocked his head. "I'm not sure."

"You said you weren't interested in expanding the house. I can't see any wife living in that cottage with children. Where would you all fit?"

"I see yer point." Ian got up and walked back to the window, then turned and faced her once again. "I want to know ye, Hope." Ian smiled. "Can we take a walk along the shore, spend some time getting to know one another?"

"Yes, that would be nice."

With quick strides Ian made his way across the room and swooped her into an embrace. "I shall pray, too."

Joy soared in Hope's heart. Goodness, she could get lost in those wonderful blue eyes. The creak of a floorboard outside in the hall brought her back to the present as she wondered which of her family members had been eavesdropping. "Good day, Mr. McGrae."

"Good day, Miss Lang."

As she watched him leave, she was already anticipating their walk. Perhaps it would be a way for them to start with a clean slate. The thought made her happier than she'd been in quite some time.

Ian raced out of the house knowing they'd been overheard for at least part of their conversation. Of course, the Langs weren't blind. It was obvious that he and Hope were entertaining the idea of a courtship.

Courtship! All of that would have been unnecessary had they followed through with the betrothal. Now they were dancing around one another, trying to get to know each other and still not feeling comfortable at all.

Ian knew one thing: Hope's embrace centered him. He felt more at peace in her arms than anywhere else. Her comments about the house and the assumptions he'd made about her convicted him again. He hadn't even given her the option of building additions for children. Admittedly, if it was only him, he'd be content. But if he had a wife and children, the cottage would be too small. No wonder she told him she'd only be content in the cottage for a while.

He walked back to the ranch, thinking and rethinking everything that was said and not said. *Father, I'm praying for me spouse. If it be Hope, help us work through our differences. Help us to listen to one another better.*

As he approached the barn he noticed the sheriff. The stern look on his face meant something wasn't right. The sheriff greeted Ian. "Mr. McGrae, there seems to be a problem concerning the ownership of your land."

"How is this possible, Sheriff? The land belonged to Mr. Sanders, who's owned it for the past forty years. Me lawyer spoke with a judge. This is makin' no sense."

Sheriff Bower leaned back against his horse. "Let's go speak with the Sanderses."

Ian walked the sheriff up to the Sanderses' farmhouse and knocked. Mrs. Sanders greeted them with an open door. In no time at all, William Sanders had all the paperwork out and proved what Ian had stated.

Sheriff Bower scratched his beard. "I have a court order here to remove you from your land, Mr. McGrae. Because the house and livestock are on the land, they belong to this owner, according to the court papers."

William leaned forward. "Sheriff, is it possible these papers are forged?"

"I'd say they require some further investigation. I'll return to town and speak with the judge who wrote the order. May I bring your copies with me?"

William glanced over to his wife. She shook her head. "Mable and I think we'd better keep these originals with all the problems going on."

"Fair enough. Would you care to join me and speak with the judge?"

"Certainly. Let me change my attire. Ian, would you ready the wagon for me and the missus?"

"Yes, sir." Ian hustled out of the house and down to the barn. He hitched up the horse to the wagon and noticed someone watching him from behind the bushes. He strode over to the house as if he hadn't seen anyone.

"Sheriff, we have another problem. Someone's watching the place."

Sheriff Bower rubbed the back of his neck. "All right

then. What I think is going on is someone is trying to rob Mr. McGrae of his livestock, and possibly more. In any event, I'll send Mr. Sanders to the judge with the warrant I received and I'll double back after we've gone down the road a bit."

William placed a protective arm around his wife. "Do you think Mable is safe?"

"I believe she's safer with you on the wagon than staying behind here," Sheriff Bower said. "Mr. McGrae, what kinds of weapons do you have at your cottage?"

"A couple of knives, Mr. Sanders's shotgun and me shepherd's crook."

"All right then, you head on to your cottage. Make certain all is in order. Bring your dogs up to the Sanderses' house and let's give this guy the impression you're obeying the order. Mr. Sanders, stop by my office and tell my deputy to get some men out here as soon as possible before you go to the judge."

"Yes, sir. Come, Mable. Be safe, Ian. They're only livestock, not worth your life," William admonished.

"Yes, sir."

But of course, his livestock were his life and his future. *Dear God, please bring wisdom to this situation.*

Ian did as directed and went to the cottage as the others left for the city. He slipped a knife into his boot then moved on to gather the puppies. How was he supposed to carry six three-week-old puppies? He could do two, maybe three at a time, if the little ones didn't squirm too much. Ian searched the cottage for a bin of some sort. Tara started prancing around. She didn't care for people messing with her babies. She also was very astute and could tell something wasn't right. Ian figured the best place for Conall was out keeping watch of the sheep.

"Oh, no, the ram!" Ian bolted toward the barn with Mr.

Sanders's shotgun in hand. He ran into the barn where he found the ram standing still, munching on his oats. He glanced at the other pen that held the ewes. They, too, were safe. What was going on here?

A carriage pulled into the yard. "Ian?" Hope's voice called out.

"Hope, what are ye doin' here?"

Her shoulders squared, she narrowed her gaze. She didn't like Ian's tone. How could it change in a couple of hours?

Ian whistled for Tara. She jumped from the cottage and ran toward him. He signaled to her to check for predators in the area. Tara immediately put her nose to the ground and moved off in a search pattern. Ian closed the distance between him and Hope.

"It isn't safe," he said. "Someone has been in the woods behind the barn."

"What?" Hope squealed.

Tara growled and yapped.

"Stay here," Ian commanded, and then he took off running toward the commotion.

Chapter 13

Hope tightened her grasp on the reins. "What's going on?" she called out, but Ian was already on the run with shotgun in hand. She scanned the area looking for anything out of place. Seeing nothing, she waited, feeling helpless, wishing she could offer Ian some assistance.

After a few minutes Ian and Tara returned. He motioned for Tara to return to the house. "What's going on?" she asked again, concerned.

Ian came up beside her and leaned on the armrest of her buggy, catching his breath. "Sheriff Bower came to remove me from the property but after a few words with the Sanderses we were able to convince him that the order was wrong. He agreed to go to the judge and investigate the matter further with the Sanderses. Then I caught someone in the woods behind the house and..." Ian stopped and turned at the sound of approaching horse hooves. The sheriff had returned.

"I thought the plan was for you to move your dogs into the Sanderses' home," the sheriff said.

"I went to check on me ram and I had Tara investigate. There was evidence of someone in the bushes behind those palm fronds. But whoever it be ran off again when Tara charged after him."

"Do you know what is going on, Sheriff?" Hope asked.

"I'm afraid not. I'll have my deputies check on you a couple of times throughout the rest of the day. Perhaps we've scared the individual off for now." The sheriff glanced back at Ian's cottage. "Your dogs are good protection."

"That they are, Sheriff."

"Good. Good day, Miss Lang. May I suggest you not travel out here on your own for the next few days? More than likely someone is after Mr. McGrae's sheep." He paused with a glance back at the cottage. "And possibly your dogs. Word around town is the pups sell for a hefty sum."

Hope's back stiffened. Had Ian made himself a target for thieves? Had his way of advertising his dogs attracted the interest of criminals in St. Augustine? But the pups wouldn't be worth the money Ian hoped to earn if he didn't have the time to train them. Plus they were still too young to leave their mother. "Good day, Sheriff."

Hope turned back to Ian as he watched the sheriff ride down the road. "Looks like you're in a real mess."

Ian turned to her and smiled a weary smile. "No more than usual since I moved to America. So, what brought ye out here, Hope?"

"You," she said after a pause. "We need to talk and I didn't want to wait any longer."

"Are ye up for a walk? I want to go to the back pasture and check on Conall and the sheep, especially with someone lurking about."

"Sure. I'm so sorry that all of this is happening to you. It's frightening." Perhaps she should have waited for their walk but she'd wanted to get this business with Hamilton Scott out of the way before they enjoyed each other's company.

"It's nothing the dogs and I can't handle," Ian assured her as he led her toward the back pasture. "Is there something ye needed to discuss with me before we stroll along the shore?" he said, his blue eyes shining.

Hope nodded, but she couldn't seem to make the words come out.

Ian took a few more steps. "I know something bad happened before I arrived and ye were hurt badly by it."

Hope nodded and swallowed. She had come out here to tell him all about Hamilton Scott, but she wasn't ready after all. He would need to gain her trust. "Yes, I was hurt badly but I wanted to let you know it was not of a romantic nature. I'll tell you the rest at another time, when I am not breaking all the rules of etiquette by being here on my own. I was counting on the Sanderses being here."

"I'm sorry ye are breaking etiquette but I'm glad ye are here. As for the other matter, I shall not pry. I will wait on ye."

Just then, Ian picked up his pace. "Look over there." He pointed toward the fence about half a mile ahead. Hope saw a bobcat lurking in the tall grass.

"Ian, don't!" she yelled but it was too late. He was already charging after it.

Ian chased after the animal. He heard Hope holler at him but he was bound and determined to keep the beast away from his flock. He reached down and picked up a hunk of jagged coral as he got closer. The bobcat watched him, coiled and hunched down in the tall grasses. Ian signaled for Conall to move the sheep away from the fence.

Conall went straight to work. The bobcat poked his head up then slunk down. He eyed Ian, poised to spring as Hope caught up to him. "Ian, don't. The best thing is to simply back away." Ian halted.

"I can't do that, Hope. He's after me flock." He fingered the rock in his hand. He wasn't close enough to get a good throw in.

"Ian, please. If you leave them alone they will retreat. If you attack they will attack you." She grabbed his arm. "Trust me, I know these animals."

He glanced at Hope. He saw worry and compassion in her green eyes. "Aye, I'll take yer advice."

"Good, now slowly walk backward."

Ian signaled to Conall, and together they walked backward.

"You're going to need to start carrying a weapon with you until you teach them this is your property and your livestock."

"Will they learn?"

"After they get shot at a few times, yes, they should move on to easier prey."

"I could top the fencing with additional barbed wire so the predators cannot jump over it."

"That would probably be wise."

As they herded the sheep back toward the house, Ian asked, "Tell me about yer new business. Why are ye doing it?"

"I felt it was time to use some of the gifts the Lord has given me." She glanced off into the distance then brought her focus back to him. "I like to sew, and I can design practical clothing for women who work."

"Women don't work…" Ian saw the fire in her eyes. He held up his hands. "I didn't mean it that way." He waited until he could see her temper drop down a few notches. "What I meant to say was most women work in the home. What would a new dress design do for them?"

Hope smiled. "You are so typical of most men. You believe women shouldn't work outside the home, and some don't even consider the chores a woman does around the house as work. But I won't pull that loose thread. What men fail to see is that women are working all around them. For example, Grace Arman works in the inn…"

"Yes, but…" Ian stopped, about to say that she did the women's work.

Hope went on. "What about Mrs. Leonardy, the butcher's wife? She handles orders, cuts meat and does just about everything her husband does in the butcher shop, plus does the housework and raising of the children."

Ian nodded. She did raise a good point.

"And what about Sandra Allen at the mercantile? She takes orders, unpacks them, loads the shelves and re-orders stock. Would you say she doesn't work?"

He raised his hands in surrender.

"That's my point. Women work all over this town. And for workingwomen like Sandra and Grace, a sharp-looking dress without as many layers of fabric is practical. I won't be setting a fashion trend, and most of my work will be consignments, designing a dress to the customer's wishes, but…"

"I understand, and ye are a hard worker. I've seen that on many occasions. What shocked me most was seeing ye doing the chambermaid work for the inn."

He could see his cottage now. The sheep were out of

danger and walking at an even pace. He signaled Conall to lead them toward the pens.

"It's not my favorite type of work but Grace is a good friend and she needed the help."

"Aye, I understand. Ye are generous. It just struck me odd that a gal with yer social standing would do it at all."

"So maybe ye had it wrong about me not being fit to be a shepherd's wife?" she teased.

Ian roared with laughter. "Ye do have a way of making yer point."

Hope curtsied. "Thank you."

"So when are we having ourselves that stroll, Hope?"

Hope smiled. "I have to admit I am afraid."

He reached out and took her hand. "I am, too. However, our God doesn't make mistakes and if we're to proceed He'll be with us." They walked hand in hand back to his cottage.

"I need to go. May I return on Monday after I'm finished with my work? I'd like to give you a hand around the ranch and talk more."

"I'd like that." He took her hand and brought it to his lips. "I should probably escort ye home, keep ye safe."

"I'll be fine. I know how to use the whip."

Ian nodded. "Until Monday." He wanted to add *me love*, but this was not the time. They had a lot of work ahead of them. He would need to be patient until she opened up and told him what had happened in the past. He sensed she wanted to but still needed to trust him. And he couldn't blame her, considering some of the rude conversations they'd had before. "Goodbye, Hope."

She leaned over and kissed him on the cheek. "Goodbye, Ian."

His heart raced as he watched her walk away.

Is it possible, Lord? Is she meant for me?

* * *

For the past three days Hope had been coming out to spend a couple of hours each day with Ian on the ranch. They worked outside where anyone could see them and each time she came, they notified the Sanderses. Each day she learned a little bit more about raising sheep while he in turn was spending time learning about her future business. She'd decided to start small but did accept a gift from her father, which was paying her rent for the first six months. Soon she wouldn't have free time to spend with Ian.

She grabbed the sketches she'd worked on last night out of her buggy and brought them to the door of Ian's cottage. "Ian?" she called as she approached.

Ian came out with a trail of puppies following him. Hope giggled. "You look like the pied piper of puppies."

"I shall blow me magic pipe and they shall follow me anywhere," he said with a wink.

"I brought the sketches I was working on last night. I took into consideration some of your thoughts on the wool and, well…" She laid the sketches on the porch table. "Tell me what you think."

Ian leaned over and examined each drawing with interest. "I like them all but I like this one the best."

Joy filled Hope to overflowing. "Thank you, it's my favorite, as well. I designed this one for Sandra Allen. It's feminine but will give her the freedom to climb ladders, fill the shelves from the storage room and still look pretty."

"Very practical."

Hope reached into her purse and pulled out a rolled paper held together with a pink ribbon. "This one is for the New York governor's wife, who will be here for another month. This dress has all the bells and whistles that the French and English designers are still encouraging this year. Plus I took a layer out to cool it down for the Southern heat. The jacket can come off and reveal a lighter dress below. See?" She pointed to another pose of the same outfit without the jacket.

"It still has the bustle."

"No respectable socialite would be caught not wearing one, no matter how impractical they think they are. Unfortunately the governor's wife is one of those people. You have to make what the customers want, not what you think would look best on them."

"Don't ye think ye have the power to persuade them?"

"Tried. Had to back down or I wouldn't have the sale."

"Aye, I understand that. Luckily that kind of customer doesn't affect me." Ian gathered the drawings and handed them back to her.

"Mother said to invite you over this evening if you can leave." Hope loved how close she and Ian were becoming. She cherished that he would take the time to go over dress designs with her, that he actually took an interest in it because it was something she enjoyed.

"I believe I can. Let me freshen up and I'll escort ye back to yer house."

"I'll wait for you in the carriage." She'd given up on walking back and forth. Her time was too precious. And while she was only saving twenty minutes, when you added in the time to hook up the horse to the buggy and then disconnect them afterward, it was still twenty minutes. Soon she wouldn't even have these few minutes with Ian. The storefront would be open for her to move into on Saturday, two days from now.

Mable Sanders walked over toward the buggy. "Hello, Hope. It is good to see you."

"And good to see you, as well, Mrs. Sanders. How have you been?"

"I've been better."

"What seems to be the problem?"

"Whoever is disputing the sale to Ian has now put a claim on our house."

"What has the sheriff said?"

"He doesn't know what to make of it. He spent the better part of a day at the registrar's office trying to figure out who might be making the claim. But he found it in the records as clear as day that the property belonged to S. H. Wilson."

"But you purchased the property forty years ago and still have the purchase and sale from the original owner."

"That's the thing. The sheriff found the records of our original purchase, as well."

"Well if this S. H. Wilson has owned the land for the past forty years, where has he been all this time and why hasn't he been paying the taxes?"

"All good questions, my dear. Not to mention, the sheriff hasn't found the man who was lurking in the bushes the other day."

Hope decided she would go to the registrar's office again tomorrow and do some of her own searching. She'd go back further, to when the Ingermansons owned the property, and follow those records back.

"Good afternoon, Mable," Ian said as he walked toward them. "How are you doing?"

"Fair. Hope can fill you in. I best get back to my laundry before the rains come."

"God bless ye, Mable." Ian climbed up into the buggy and took the reins. "What happened?"

"This land mess." Hope went on to explain everything Mrs. Sanders had told to her. "I'm going to the registrar's office tomorrow to do a bit more research. There's something familiar about this S. H. Wilson but I can't put my finger on it."

"I'll join ye. When will ye be going there?"

"How's two thirty?"

"I'll be there." The buggy bounced as one of the wheels hit a deep rut. Hope banged into Ian. Ian steadied the buggy and wrapped his arm around her. "Are ye all right?"

Hope gazed into his crystal-blue eyes. She was drawn to him like no other. She glanced down to his lips. Ian leaned in to kiss her. Hope closed her eyes in anticipation.

"Not now, me love. Soon, when we are in private. Others are watching."

Chapter 14

Ian fought down every straining desire to kiss Hope. He couldn't take advantage of her when so many were aware of them. If it were simply his honor, he'd kiss her. But Hope's honor was far more precious to him.

Hope opened her dazzling green eyes.

"I love yer eyes." He wanted to move forward in their relationship but was concerned as to whether or not he should. "They remind me of Ireland."

Hope raised her eyebrows.

"They do," he defended. "They remind me of the rich green hills. I spent many a day in those hills tending the sheep." *And I'd like to spend the rest of my days looking into those eyes.* Ian straightened. It was the first time he'd admitted to himself that he wanted to spend the rest of his life with Hope.

Hope slid away from him in the buggy. They rode the rest of the way to her home in silence. He pulled into the carriage house. "I'll take care of the horse."

Ian helped Hope down. "I'm sorry. I wanted to kiss you but there were too many people watching."

Hope nibbled her lower lip. Ian reached up and caressed her silky smooth skin. "Ye are beautiful, Hope."

She smiled.

"May I kiss ye now?" Hope's eyes widened.

"I would prefer ye didn't," Drake Lang's voice boomed.

Ian pulled away and stood ramrod straight. "I'm sorry, sir. It won't…" He was going to say it wouldn't happen again but knew he could not resist kissing Hope and planned on kissing her as soon as possible.

"Hope, go help your mother. Mr. McGrae and I have a few things to discuss."

"Papa, no. If it involves me, I should be here."

Drake put his hands on his daughter's shoulders. "I will speak with ye later. This is something a father must do."

Hope nodded. Drake pulled her into a tender embrace then released her. After she left, Drake's piercing gaze met Ian's. Ian locked his gazed on Mr. Lang. "I'm sorry if I've offended ye, sir."

Drake placed his hands behind his back and started to pace in the carriage house. "Ye are putting me in a position I do not wish to be in."

"How so, sir?"

"I know Hope has been at your ranch. When ye were in need and Hope was doing her Christian charity, I was not concerned. But now that ye and she are showing signs of…interest, I am quite concerned."

"I will not dishonor Hope, sir."

"But ye already are in some circles, Mr. Lang. I will not allow that."

Ian couldn't imagine not seeing Hope again. But he wasn't ready to commit himself to her, either. It was too soon. "Mr. Lang, Hope and I bring out the worst in each other. But I believe we also will bring out the best. Unfortunately, we are not there yet. And I don't know any other way of discovering how to bring harmony in our friendship without spending time with one another."

Drake rubbed his beard. "Ye can spend time here at the house, or in public, but not at your farm. It is not proper and I will not have my daughter's reputation ruined."

"Sir, if I may speak frankly, ye have blessed her most—if not all—of her life. She's never wanted for anything. But I am a simple man with simple needs. I do not wish to be the owner of a large plantation and have me servants do all me work. The question is, can she live like that?"

Drake regarded him carefully. "Take care of the horse. I need to speak with my daughter."

"Yes, sir."

Ian knew Mr. Lang was not satisfied and there was no question he would need to speak with Hope and hear her side.

Ian went to work removing the harness from the horse. He led the animal to his stall and brushed him down, then set out some fresh oats. Was he really ready to court Hope? And if so, who would he get to be their chaperone, especially when they were simply doing chores at the ranch?

Ian leaned against the stall wall. If only they hadn't broken their betrothal. They would be married and working out these details. Then again, maybe Hope wouldn't be seeking her own business venture, and maybe his eyes wouldn't have opened to the possibility of a wife working apart from the home.

America was changing him. Or was it that incred-

ible redhead? In either case, he wasn't ready to go into
the house just yet. Ian pushed away from the stable wall
and headed into town. He needed to give them time. *He*
needed time.

"Papa, how could you?" Hope demanded.

Her father squared his shoulders. "How could I not,
Hope? I can see what's going on."

Her mother came up beside her and wrapped her arms
around her. Gabe, who had come in with his mother,
fled. "Hope, go to yer room and give me a moment with
yer father."

Hope obeyed, knowing her mother understood her
feelings for Ian. Hope knew her father; he would demand a formal courtship. There would be chaperones.
She would not be allowed to go to Ian's ranch alone any
longer.

And perhaps her father was right. Did they have a
chance of becoming happy as husband and wife? It was
too soon to know. If her passions were the only test then
yes, they would be a happily married couple. However,
she worried she couldn't trust her emotions. They had led
her astray one too many times over the years.

"Hope, would you come down here, darling?" her
mother eventually called from the bottom of the stairs.

Hope obeyed and went into the family parlor. Her father stood at the fireplace with his arm on the mantel.
"Yes, sir?"

"First," her mother started, "please tell your father and
me what your feelings are for Mr. McGrae."

"Confused. I like him. We're attracted—" she bowed
her head and looked toward her lap "—to one another,
and I've never felt like this before. But neither of us is
sure we are right for one another. Which is why I've been

spending time with him, to see if we have a chance at a possible relationship."

Her father cleared his throat. "This would not be an issue if ye hadn't broken the betrothal."

"I know. However, I wouldn't be starting my own business if I had married Ian right away. He wouldn't have seen me as anything more than a shepherd's wife. Now he's learning that I have a brain and know how to use it. He's actually been learning things from me, as I have been learning from him. Don't you see? We are learning about each other so we can develop toward…"

Drake Lang relaxed his stance, came over and sat beside Hope on the sofa. "I am concerned, daughter. I've let ye do more than most women are allowed. People talk, they have always talked. But yer honor has always been protected. I can't allow ye and Mr. McGrae to ruin yer honor just to find out if ye want to marry one another. I will insist on a formal courtship."

Hope closed her eyes. "No, Papa, please don't. I would not want to wait a year to marry Ian, if we should decide to marry."

"Drake—" her mother respectfully interjected.

Drake held up a hand. "Sally, it will have to be courtship or betrothal. I can't have Hope's reputation soiled."

Her mother reached over and placed her hand on her father's. Drake closed his eyes. Hope watched her mother stroke her father's hand with her thumb, a silent communication developed over the years with one another.

"Papa, please try to understand. For the past three days I've been going over to the ranch, and Ian's been teaching me about the sheep, how to care for them, how to market them, all kinds of things. And I've been teaching him about the business I'm working on. We've been working together and it's been wonderful. Ian's from the old country—he's just beginning to see how and where his mother helped his father on the farm. We need this time. I'm too independent to simply be a shepherd's wife."

"Sally, speak to your daughter!" Her father restrained himself from speaking further.

"I'm sorry, Drake," her mother said. "Ye need to listen." She turned toward Hope. "Has Ian been a gentleman?"

"Ian is a perfect gentleman," Hope insisted. There was no need to tell her father about the one kiss they had shared that Ian so deeply regretted, feeling he had compromised her honor.

"At least the boy has some sense," her father mumbled.

"Yes, Papa, more than me at times," Hope admitted. There was a knock at the front door.

"That'll be Ian," Drake said. "Come in," he called.

Hope's heart stopped in her chest. The moment of truth had arrived.

Ian squared his shoulders and stepped into the Langs' house. It was time to face Hope's parents. He'd marry her if that's what Drake Lang insisted he do, not that he hadn't had similar thoughts. But he doubted Hope would agree. There was still something she was holding back from him, and he did not want to push her.

Gabe ushered Ian into the parlor then left him with Hope and her parents. Hope stood at the fireplace. He came up beside her. He wanted to wrap her in his arms but knew that wouldn't be prudent.

Drake cleared his throat. "Mr. McGrae, we've been talking about the position you and Hope have found yourselves in. Hope is not ready to commit to marriage. Are ye?"

Ian looked at Hope. "I am not certain it would be the

best situation for Hope. Yer daughter is a fascinating person. I have never met another woman… No, let me rephrase that. I have never met *anyone* quite like her before." Ian turned back to her parents. "Forgive me, what are ye asking of me?"

Drake stood and walked up to Ian. "For the next couple of weeks would ye only meet me daughter in a public setting or here at the house? After that, we shall talk once again. At that point we shall decide how to proceed."

"Yes, sir."

Drake turned and faced his daughter. "Hope?"

She nodded.

"Sally, let us leave these two to discuss in private." Drake took his wife's hand and led her out of the parlor.

Ian turned and faced Hope. She was angry, or maybe not angry as much as frustrated. "I'm sorry, sweetheart."

"Don't you go calling me sweetheart after all of this."

"Hope." He engulfed her in his embrace. "Please, I understand the humiliation of all this but yer parents are right, it isn't good for yer honor to be alone with me all the time. I will be the first to admit I like having ye at me side. But there is something you're not telling me. Until ye can…"

She turned in his arms and faced him. "I'm sorry, Ian."

"Oil and water, me dear." He winked.

She snuggled her face into his chest. He held her with compassion.

"Then we are agreed, we shall do as yer parents have asked and only meet in public for a couple of weeks." He kissed her forehead.

She took in a deep pull of air and released it slowly. "All right. Do you still want to meet me at the registrar's office tomorrow?"

"Yes, it is public." He smiled.

Hope chuckled. "You cannot spend too much time away from the ranch."

"No, but I can ask Mr. and Mrs. Sanders to be our official chaperones if ye come to the ranch."

"Father would agree to them." Hope stepped away. "Why does this have to be so hard?"

"Our decision to break our betrothal was a good thing, Hope. I do not know if we shall marry one day but I do know that if we do, it will be a better marriage."

Hope turned and smiled. "Yes, I think it would be."

"Come, sit with me and tell me more about this storefront and if ye are planning on hiring anyone to work with ye." Perhaps he should consider doing the same. It would give him time to visit with Hope if someone was working at the ranch.

"I would love to hire some women…"

"What about men?" he teased.

Hope laughed. "No man would listen to me. But if there was one who would, I'd hire him."

"And I might have to hire a chaperone." Ian laughed.

"The shop is a public place." She winked.

Ian fixed his eyes on her. "Then I shall visit there from time to time."

"I was thinking earlier today that soon we won't be spending too much time together, once I open my shop."

"I know, but we'll make the most out of the time we have."

Ian returned to his ranch with the desire to hire someone. But if he hired a ranch hand he'd have to increase his profits. On the other hand, he wanted the freedom to join Hope for dinner, to visit her at her shop, to pursue a life that was more than shepherding. How could he have gotten it so wrong? A shepherd's life was simple and yet, he was discovering, not all that simple. His father had both hired hands and his sons to work the ranch.

That settles it, he decided. *Tomorrow I'll start spreading the word.*

Conall pranced anxiously back and forth, alert to danger and watching over the herd. Ian pushed open the door to his house.

Papers lay scattered on the floor. Tara cowered under the bed with her puppies. He counted...there were still six. Someone had ransacked his home looking for something...but what?

Chapter 15

Hope couldn't believe what had happened last night. She and Ian were now officially courting. Well, not officially, but they were in a relationship.

Hope glanced at the clock on the mantel. She was due to meet Ian at the registrar's office in fifteen minutes. "Mum, I'll be back. I have to run to the registrar's office."

"Ye be careful. I don't mind telling ye that yer father and I are worried about this snooping ye and Ian will be doing."

"Nothing will happen, Mother." Hope had to admit she was a bit concerned about the process, as well. Someone working in the office was altering documents to make changes to persuade the courts to rule in their favor. Father had gone to Sheriff Bower earlier in the morning with regard to the name S. H. Wilson.

Hope walked to the town hall and was surprised to see the sheriff speaking with Ian.

"Miss Lang." He took a step forward. "Your father told me you were going to investigate. I have come to say, I won't stop you but I want you to report to me any of your findings. It is a good thing that you frequent this office to do research for your father's investments. You are a known person. However, Mr. McGrae is not. My concern is for your safety."

"Mr. McGrae will be with me. I should be safe and not a cause for anyone's concern."

The sheriff touched the brim of his hat. "Be careful, Miss Lang."

"I will, Sheriff."

He nodded to Ian and went on back to his office. "I should have asked him if he's heard of S. H. Wilson."

Ian reached over and held her elbow. "After we search the records. I'm curious if this kind of a situation has gone on before."

"Perhaps. But I really want to know who S. H. Wilson is." Hope followed Ian's lead. There had to be something at the town clerk's office she could find to prove the Sanderses' rightful ownership. Hope prayed she could find the missing piece to solve this problem.

"What's going on behind those pretty eyes of yers?"

Hope blinked back to the present. "Nothing. We should look to see if Wilson's name is on any other documents."

They entered the registrar's office. "Good morning, Miss Lang, how can I help you today?" asked Harold Swain, the town clerk. Harold had been working for the city for as long as Hope could remember. She couldn't imagine him being involved in this.

"I need to look at the records from 1830 through 1835."

"That's going back a ways. Let me fetch them for you." Harold left toward the records room.

Ian leaned in closer. "Why five years?"

"To ward off suspicion. I've often looked through several years with regard to the same property when researching for my father."

Ian nodded. Harold walked back in. "Would you like to sit at a desk, Miss Lang?"

"Thank you, that would be nice. May I have an extra chair for Mr. McGrae?"

"Certainly. McGrae, ain't you the fella from Ireland with those dogs?"

"Yes, sir."

"Pleasure to meet you, Mr. McGrae." Harold extended his hand. "You bought William Sanders's place, right?"

"Some of it, yes, sir."

"The Sanderses are good folk. Well, don't let me go rattling on. You young folk have work to do." Harold escorted Hope to an unused desk. Ian grabbed a chair from another desk and set it beside hers.

She opened to November 3, 1831, the date William purchased his ranch, according to his records. She traced her finger down the lines searching for the right date. Sure enough, the purchase was there in black and white. Hand-scrawled like every other entry before and after the Sanderses' purchase. "It's here, Ian," she whispered.

Ian leaned in and looked over her shoulder. "Aye, thank the Good Lord it be there."

Billy Newman, assistant town clerk, came into the office and stopped short. "Miss Lang, what can I do for you?"

"Mr. Swain got the records I needed. Thank you, Mr. Newman." Billy's complexion blanched. "Forgive my manners, Mr. Newman. This is Ian McGrae."

Billy's hand shook as he reached it out toward Ian's. "How do you do?"

"Pleasure to meet you, Mr. Newman."

"Call me Billy, everyone else does." Billy glanced over at the wall clock.

Suddenly Hope could feel in the pit of her stomach that Billy Newman knew something about Ian's property and the claim being made on it.

"Forgive me, I left some paperwork in my wagon." Billy scurried out of the office.

"What was that all about?" Ian asked. "Is he always like that?"

"No, I think he knows something." Hope closed the book she'd been going through and brought them all to Mr. Swain's office. She tapped on the glass window on his door. He looked up from the paperwork on his desk and smiled.

He stood up and made his way to the door. "That was quick."

"Has the sheriff spoken with you about Mr. McGrae's property?"

"No, but I do remember seeing a note from Ben Greeley about a mix-up on the plot numbers. I had Billy take care of that. Easy fix. Why? What's going on?"

"Mr. Swain," Ian said. "Would ye please come with us to the sheriff's office? There's a private matter we need to discuss."

Harold raised his right eyebrow. He glanced from Ian to Hope. Hope nodded. "All right, let me get my coat. I'll leave a note for Billy."

"May I take this 1831 ledger with us, as well?" Hope asked.

"No, but I'll take it." He winked. "Can't have you being responsible for items under my care."

Hope smiled. "Of course not."

Billy hadn't returned by the time Mr. Swain was ready to go, so he locked the door behind him. Within minutes they were sitting in front of the sheriff with Mr. Swain. Hope laid out her suspicions and showed the sheriff that the property was sold to the Sanderses on the exact date as their papers stated.

"And you had no idea Mr. McGrae's property was being disputed?" the sheriff asked Mr. Swain.

"No, sir. I'll be happy to look through all the records in the past year," Mr. Swain offered.

The sheriff stood up. "All right, Miss Lang, Mr. Mc-Grae, leave the rest of this investigation in my hands. I'll keep you informed once I have it all sorted out."

"But, Sheriff…" Hope started, but stopped when Ian rested his hands on her shoulders. "Yes, sir." She amended her response. "Oh, one more thing, Sheriff. A few weeks ago I was in the registrar's office and some men were talking. And someone, it sounded like Billy Newman, said, 'I'm tellin' ya, H.W., you're askin' for trouble. You can't pull this off. The judge has already asked for proof.' At the time I didn't think it had anything to do with Mr. McGrae's problems but now… Of course, he didn't specifically mention the name S. H. Wilson."

"Thank you, Miss Lang. I'll keep that in mind. You and Mr. McGrae should go now."

Hope fought off every desire to run back to the clerk's office and demand that Billy tell what he knew. Then again, it wasn't her place. Sheriff Bower was more than capable. Ian extended his elbow. Hope placed her hand in the crook and peace washed over her. It felt right.

"Thank ye, Sheriff. If Billy is involved I believe we may have come to the end of this mystery."

"I hope you're right, Mr. McGrae. However, I suspect you are not the only person to have been targeted. I intend to apprehend those involved and charge them to the full extent of the law."

"Thank ye, Sheriff. Mr. Swain, I appreciate yer help." Ian placed his hand on Hope's and led her out of the sheriff's office. "The sheriff is right, this is his matter now. But I do want to thank ye for all yer help, Hope. I don't know if we'd ever have figured out what was going on."

"But we still don't know what is going on."

"We know enough for now. We can assume that Billy Newman is in business with this S. H. Wilson fella."

"But why? Why you? What did they hope to gain from all of this?"

"Money, property, who knows? Does it really matter?"

"Yes." She was delightful when flustered.

Ian smiled.

"What?"

"Nothing. You're adorable."

Hope groaned. "Don't start with that, not now, not after the lecture last night."

"What lecture? I thought yer parents were very understanding. Back in Ireland I might find meself at the other end of a shotgun standing before the minister and a bride."

Hope giggled. "Father would never do that."

"Don't test him, darlin'. He's Irish. And we Irish tend to be…"

"As if I didn't know about ye Irish?"

Ian smiled. "No, sweetheart, ye know all too well about the Irish." He wiggled his eyebrows. "Now, why don't ye show me that storefront where ye are going to be moving into tomorrow."

Hope led him through the streets to a building not far from the main business area. She pointed through the windows. "What do you think?"

"I think ye have a lot of cleanup to do."

"The previous tenant hadn't paid their rent for a couple of months so they didn't leave under the best of circumstances. Tomorrow I move in and can start to clean and set up the place."

"If I can lend ye a hand, I will."

"Thank you."

"Let's go to Pedro's. I want to share with ye something I was thinking about last night." Ian held out his arm. Hope slid her hand in the crook of his elbow.

Hope kept pace as he led her toward the old city gates, toward Pedro's, the small Cuban restaurant. They were seated by Maria, Pedro's wife. "What may I get you, Miss Lang? Mr. McGrae?"

"The house special for me," Ian said.

"I'll have the same." Hope smiled. "And a tall glass of iced tea."

"Tea I have, but the ice delivery has not come yet." Maria apologized.

"Water with lime will be fine." Maria nodded and left their table.

Ian reached across the table and opened his hand. Hope placed her delicate hand within his. "Hope, I'm going to hire at least one, possibly two people to help me at the ranch."

"Can you afford that?"

He rubbed her silky fingers with his thumb. "It will be hard to do it this year, but I can't ignore me ranch, and I want to see ye."

Maria came up to the table with their beverages. "Miss Lang, I hear you are going to start a dress shop with clothing for the workingwoman in mind."

"Yes, I move into the shop tomorrow but it will be next week before I can open for business. Why do you ask?"

"I'm in need of a new skirt for work."

Hope gave Maria the address. She left and Ian recaptured her gaze. "Hope, what happened with Hamilton Scott?"

"Ian," Hope whispered. "It is more embarrassing than anything else. As you know, I pride myself on being thorough with regard to numbers and research. While I was working for him, I discovered some forms that had numbers out of order on a customer's property lot. I fixed them and got fired for doing it without Mr. Hamilton's permission. I thought I was doing my job. I thought I was being thorough. I did not believe I was interfering with his business..."

"I'm at a loss as to why this bothered you so."

"I was fired immediately. Then he started to ask me to pay for his loss, which he said was substantial. It didn't make sense. He belittled me, accused me of falsifying records." Hope shook her head and looked down at her lap.

Ian caressed the top of her hand with his thumb. "Hope, ye are an incredible woman. Of course ye did the right thing. And Mr. Scott was a fool not to see it. A man would be foolish not to listen to ye in business or in life." He paused. "I know I said I wasn't ready but..."

"Are you suggesting..." Her words trailed off.

"Yes, can we reactivate our betrothal? Can we get married right away? I don't want to take weeks, months, or even years to get to know ye before we marry. I want to learn as we make our way through marriage."

"What about my work?"

"Ye can work as long as ye would like. I will do what I can to support ye. I want ye to be happy but I do want a wife who will be willing to sacrifice for me, as well."

"What kind of sacrifice?"

"Time...to spend time together. I'd want ye to cook our meals, although I'll be happy to cook if I know in advance ye need to work late. I want ye in me life. I want to grow as a man with ye. The Proverbs 31 lady did many wondrous things and her husband and family were proud of her. They felt loved and cherished. That is all I ask, that ye would cherish me as much as I cherish ye."

"Oh, Ian, I do love you." Her brilliant green eyes sparkled and opened her soul down to her heart. He could see the genuine love she had for him. He prayed she could see the same love in his eyes. "Aye, I love ye, too. Shall we do this?"

Hope looked down at her plate. "It would stop all the problems Father was concerned about if we were married."

Ian held down his chuckle. "Sweetheart, if we were married, there would not be any problem with ye spending time alone with yer husband." He squeezed her hand.

Maria came up with their plates. "Forgive me." Maria's cheeks brightened with a tinge of pink.

Ian released Hope's hand and pulled his back.

Hope gazed at him but didn't speak. Maria placed the dishes down on the table and left.

"Hope?" Fear washed over Ian. Perhaps he shouldn't have been so open and frank with her. "Sweetheart?"

"Yes, I think we should reactivate our betrothal."

Ian's smile widened. Hope's fears dissipated. "How do we proceed? I don't know how all this betrothal stuff works," she said.

"I don't know, either, but we do know who does."

Hope's eyes widened. "Father?"

"Aye. Has he ever taken ye out to the woodshed? How long before I'll be able to sit?"

Hope laughed. She couldn't help herself. She could picture her father out by the side of the carriage house with a leather belt in hand. She and Gabe had received their fair share of discipline when they were younger. "Well, if he's as strong as when we were kids, it will be a week at least."

Ian chuckled, his dazzling blue eyes catching hers again. "Ye are worth it." He started to eat. His eyes went wide. He grabbed the linen napkin and wiped his brow. "What is this?"

Hope glanced down at his meal. "Fried, stuffed jalapeño peppers. They're hot." Hope bit off half of a pepper and swallowed it.

Ian grabbed Hope's water and gulped it down. Then he motioned for Maria. She retreated into the kitchen and came out with a glass of milk. Hope held back her giggles.

"Can I have something mild, please?" Ian handed his plate back.

Maria handed him the milk. "Drink, it will cool your mouth."

Ian obeyed. He drank half the glass then set it down. "How can ye eat those things?"

"I've grown up with them. Most dishes I don't like too spicy, but I do love the fried jalapeños. Especially these, when they fill them with cheese before they fry them."

Ian wagged his head. "I shall not be eating those again." His eyes were still watering. "And ye like these?"

"It's an acquired taste."

"I shall not be acquiring." He wiped his brow with his cloth napkin then sipped some more milk, moaning in gratitude as it cooled his mouth and throat down.

"Ian, are we doing the right thing?" Hope asked as she fiddled with her napkin.

"Hope, I've been praying for me spouse, and every time I do I see ye."

Hope lifted her gaze and stared into his eyes. Warmth flooded over her as he reached out and held both her hands. "The same happens to me."

The delicate smile on Hope's pink lips tickled him deep inside. "Do ye want to wait? Start a formal courtship?"

"Oh my, no. I mean," she stammered, "no, I don't want to start a formal courtship. If you haven't figured it out by now, I am not what you would call a typical woman of high social standing. I would like to have a church wedding, and I would need to make my gown, but I can sew something together within a week if I have the materials."

"A church wedding is most acceptable to me, as well. The Lord should be center in our lives." Ian reached out both his hands. "Let's pray."

Warmth flowed through her hands to his and traveled up to his heart. Hope was the right woman for him. He was glad they hadn't gotten married upon his arrival. He wouldn't have opened his eyes to the possibility of a wife being more than what he had supposed one to be. In Hope he saw the potential to have a real helpmate, someone equal to him. "Ye are going to make a great wife."

"And you will make a good husband. A man I can trust. A man who will encourage me and help keep me on the right path. Like earlier in the sheriff's office. Your hand on my shoulder to calm me down and help me see it was not my job but the sheriff's to find and apprehend the men involved with this real-estate scam."

Ian smiled and caressed the top of her hands with his thumb. He bowed his head. "Father, we are asking Ye to make it clear if we are to marry right away or wait for a season. We thank Ye for being patient with us while we argued and complained about our parents manipulating our lives. We want to make Ye the center of our home, our relationship and our future. Thank Ye for giving each of us the beautiful gift of love for one another. In Jesus's name, amen."

Hope cleared her throat. "And Father—" Ian noticed she continued to bow her head "—I want to thank You for helping us uncover the truth about Ian's land. And I too want to thank You for Your patience and for guiding us through these difficult days. Even if it was our own folly making them difficult. In Jesus's name, amen."

"Amen." Ian released Hope and noticed Maria was standing by their table, waiting.

"I'm sorry I keep interrupting you two while you are having such a private conversation. But here is your meal, Mr. McGrae, and I won't tell anyone, except Pedro, of course, but congratulations."

Hope smiled and put a finger to her lips. "My parents don't know yet."

Maria closed her lips, twisted her fingers in front of her mouth as if she were turning a key. "My lips are sealed." She winked.

Ian looked down at his plate. This was more like it. Cuban beef with a side of plantains, black beans and rice. "This is a meal…not those things."

Hope laughed and popped another jalapeño into her mouth.

After the meal, they walked toward her house. It was time to consult with her parents, and after last night Hope was not too sure how they would react. "I'm worried about my father."

"How so?" Ian snuggled closer as they walked in the

traditional way of a gentleman escorting a lady, but anyone on the street could tell they were in love.

In love! It was hard to believe that after all this time she'd finally met someone she loved. Not that twenty-one was that old. And to think it was the very man whom her parents had agreed she would marry one day. "Last night we told them that neither one of us were ready to get married. Now we're coming to them, less than twenty-four hours later, to tell them we want to get married. I don't think Father will let us marry as quickly as you would like."

"I will do whatever is required, whether it is waiting for a year and enduring a proper courtship or marrying ye tonight. I do love ye, Hope. No matter how foolishly I behaved. But I think it was good that we didn't get together right away. I wouldn't have discovered how to encourage ye to be more than a simple shepherd's wife."

"And I do want to be your wife, fully and completely. But you are right, I also want to design clothing. It will add a little income for the family."

"I don't believe we will need the extra…" He caught himself as Hope squared her shoulders. Ian placed his finger on her lips. "Let a man finish. I don't believe we will need the extra. However, we can use it for vacations, travel, the children, whatever we decide is a good expense for our family."

Hope smiled. "You do know how to turn this girl's heart."

Their conversation was broken by the cheerful greeting of a familiar voice. "Hope, Ian!" Grace Arman called out.

The couple looked down the road to see her walking toward them in slow, measured steps.

"Grace, what are you doing out here?" Hope asked as she ran to her friend's side. "Is everything all right?"

"I'm fine. The baby is fine. I'm starting my fifth month, and Dr. Peck says I'm safe to get up and about, although I can't exert myself too much." Grace motioned with her eyes over to Ian, posing a question in the silent language shared between close girlfriends. Hope smiled and nodded. Grace engulfed her in a hug. "I was coming to see your mother for some fresh herbs."

"Oh." Hope glanced over to Ian.

"Bad timing?" Grace asked.

Ian came up beside her and placed his hands on her shoulders. "Is Mrs. Lang expecting ye?"

"No."

"Then would ye be so kind as to give us thirty minutes with them before ye visit?" Ian pleaded.

Grace smiled. "Absolutely. I'll go sit down in Memorial Park." Then she added, "Congratulations."

Hope's cheeks flamed. Grace chuckled as she crossed the road and headed for the park. "How does she know?" Ian asked.

"The foolish grin on your face might be a clue," Hope teased.

"And what about ye?"

"I'm an open book. Come, let's face my parents."

"It won't be that bad."

They entered the house and found her father at the counter next to her mother, who was dishing out his lunch. "Mum, Papa," Hope called out. They turned toward the radiant couple then exchanged glances with one another.

"How did yer search at the registrar's office go?" her father asked.

Ian answered. "Good. We found that Mr. Newman

has been conspiring with S. H. Wilson. Sheriff Bower and Mr. Swain will be following up and tracking down any other victims."

"Excellent. I'm glad that mess is nearly over."

Hope glanced up at Ian. Ian cleared his throat. "Mr. Lang, Hope and I were wondering what it would take to reactivate the betrothal."

Before Drake could respond, Hope rushed to explain their sudden decision. "It's really quite practical…it would solve so many problems…and look how you and Mum…"

"Let me put ye two out of your misery. Your mother and I discussed it last night and we felt that perhaps ye would come to the same conclusion. However, we did expect it to take another week or two." Drake Lang crossed his arms over his chest. "When are ye hoping to marry?"

Ian looked down at Hope then back to her father. "A couple of weeks. Hope will need that time to sew her bridal gown. We'd like a church wedding," Ian added.

Hope reached over and took her father's hand. "Papa, whenever it is good for you and Mum. We are agreeable to whatever is best for everyone."

"What of your parents, Ian? Would they not like to come?" her mother asked.

"My parents love me very much but they said they would not come to America. Their home is in Ireland and they don't plan on leaving it, even for a visit."

Her mother nodded. Hope knew she'd heard stories from her parents' own family members who felt the same way. "I understand. Ye must decide, Drake. But do make it soon." Sally winked at her husband.

"Fine." Mr. Lang pulled out a pocket pad and flipped through a couple of pages. "How about next Saturday? If the pastor is free."

"That be fine with me, sir." Ian turned to Hope. "Sweetheart, I do not want to leave ye but I must tend to me sheep. They've been alone for hours."

"I'll take care of notifying the pastor. Small wedding, right? Just family and a few friends?"

"Could we do a barbecue on me ranch, like when they built me house?"

Sally lit up. "What a marvelous idea. Drake will pay for all the food. We'll get Mable to help. She did such a wonderful job the last time. Would you ask Mable and William to come to our house later today to help us plan?"

"Yes, ma'am." Ian bent over and kissed Hope on the cheek. "I'll come as soon as I can. I love ye," he whispered. His breath brushed across her face.

"I love you, too." Hope watched as Ian raced down the hall then turned to see her parents with their all-knowing grins. "It's all your fault," she teased. "You've been praying for him since he was five."

Drake and Sally roared with laughter.

Chapter 16

Ian worked day and night trying to get ahead of his duties on the ranch so he could take a few days off after the wedding. Hope had been doing pretty much the same. She worked constantly, cleaning up the shop in order to make her wedding gown, which he couldn't wait to see. They postponed the shop's public opening until after their wedding trip: a steamboat ride down the St. Johns River.

Mrs. Sanders was in her glory helping to plan the wedding dinner. Everyone who had come out for the build was invited, along with a few others related to the Lang family and their business. The hardest part was to accept Drake Lang's gift of an additional room being put on his cottage as his wedding present to them. But he made a logical argument that if his daughter was to have the kind of wedding expected within his social standing, he would be paying more than the cost of the small addition.

Ian washed up with a quick dip in the river after putting out fresh oats for the sheep.

Gabe came up with one of his friends, Daniel Webber, who had a four-year-old son. Daniel said he'd watch over the ranch while Ian and Hope took their honeymoon trip down the St. Johns River. Oddly enough, he had seen more of Florida than Hope, who had been born and raised there. "Evening, Gabe, Daniel. Where's Mikey?"

"He's raiding Mrs. Sanders's cookie jar." Ian smiled. He'd been favored with some of those cookies and knew they would satisfy any sweet tooth.

"I'm here for my next lesson, Ian," Daniel said.

Ian went over the final steps in the care and feeding of his sheep with Daniel for the next hour. "Any questions?"

Daniel grabbed the tool for cleaning their hooves. "The axial wall cleaning is all I'll have to do?"

"Correct. I've trimmed their toes, heels and soles so they are fine for a while. What about the commands for the dogs?"

Daniel went over the basic commands. "Excellent. I really appreciate your willingness to help out in this way. Now remember, don't let Mikey spoil the puppies. He can run and play with them but he can't feed them treats."

"I understand, and I believe Mikey understands."

"Good. I know it sounds harsh but it's what makes me dogs workers, not pets."

"Come now, I've seen how you love your dogs, Ian," Gabe teased.

"Of course I do, but that's only after they've earned it."

"I'm glad God doesn't ask us to earn it." Daniel smiled. "I'd still be trying and failing."

Ian chuckled and added, "I'd be right behind ye, Daniel. Are ye good to stay with the animals for a couple of hours so I can see me bride to be? I believe I need to have me suit fitted."

Daniel laughed. "It's an experience."

Gabe chuckled. "The first time a man is fitted for clothing is an experience. Just remember, the gentleman is only measuring your pant leg."

Ian knitted his eyebrows then widened them. "Oh."

"Exactly."

"I hear the sheep. I think they need me."

Gabe grabbed Ian and pulled him toward the wagon. "See ya later, Dan."

Daniel laughed and waved.

Humiliation—that was what marriage was—humiliation. Perhaps not marriage but certainly the wedding-in-a-church part. Ian didn't realize how much humiliation until he'd been fitted and readied for his three-piece suit with tails and a top hat. Ian tugged at the tight starched collar. "Mr. McGrae." The tailor slapped his hand. "Stay still."

"I'm sorry."

Gabe snickered. Mr. Lang turned his back toward Ian. "I can't wait until it is yer turn, Gabe."

"If I'm fortunate one day, I hope so."

Ian smiled. "Aye, I am the fortunate one."

Mr. Lang turned and faced him. "That ye are, son. Me daughter is a rare gem."

"Aye, that she is. And she's worth all this fussing."

"Good." Drake brushed his hand on the sleeve of his coat.

"Gabe, ye do this willingly a couple of times a year?" Ian laughed. "No man needs that much clothing."

"It's my weakness," Gabe admitted.

There was a tap on the plate glass window of the shop. Ian glanced over. Hope's fiery red hair glowed.

He smiled. She gave him a thumbs-up. She approved; the last thirty minutes of torture were well worth it.

She came in. "That's the phoniest smile I've ever seen you make." Hope giggled.

Gabe and Mr. Lang joined in her jocularity. Ian couldn't resist. "Ah, me love, ye know me so well."

Ian was happy to be joining this family. He missed his own but the Langs were good people who understood the value of life as well as the value of money.

"Mum said that if you have time, she has supper for you."

"I don't know." Ian turned to Gabe. "Ye know Daniel, would he mind if I was late?"

"Don't know. You could send a courier to let him know." Gabe rubbed the back of his neck.

"I'll take care of it. You are a little pinned right now," Hope offered.

"And ye are going to do this to women? I didn't know ye were a sadist."

The tailor cleared his throat.

"Me apologies, sir." The heat on Ian's face felt like he'd been out in the hot Florida sun with no protection for days.

Hope laughed. "Just remember you're doing this for me." She winked. "I'll send a message and have the courier come back with a reply."

"Thank ye." He turned, the tailor's needle stuck him. "Sorry."

Ian groaned.

After dinner, Hope rode with Ian back to his ranch so she could take home Daniel and Michael. The entire family had spent the evening joking and teasing one another, and Ian fit right in with the mix. Hope slid closer and snuggled with him.

"It is a good thing we be married in a few days."

Hope giggled. "I'm looking forward to it."

A horse and rider came up beside them. "Mr. Mc-Grae, Miss Lang," Sheriff Bower called out. Ian pulled the reins for the horse to stop.

"I'm glad I caught up with you. I wanted to report on the problems you were facing with your land purchase. Billy Newman confessed. He and Hamilton Scott worked together to defraud several folks with these false land claims. They would write a false title of land ownership, then threaten the owners with court action, as they did with you, Mr. McGrae. Then Mr. Scott, acting as S. H. Wilson, would ask for a small—or not so small—fee to give the false title of the land to the rightful owners. It worked several times. I'm hoping to recover the funds from the others who were swindled. But for now Mr. Newman and Mr. Scott are behind bars waiting for the judge." The sheriff leaned back in his saddle and smiled. "The honorable Judge Paige will be presiding over their trial. His name was forged by Mr. Scott or Mr. Newman at least once."

"Hamilton Scott?" Hope's voice faltered. "Is it true, Sheriff?"

"He denies the charges, but according to Mr. Newman, he's the one. Didn't you work for him at one point?"

"Yes, sir."

"Did you know about this?"

"No, sir. I would have told you if I knew."

Ian placed a loving hand on her knee. "Hope, Gabe said ye were fired falsely. Could that have anything to do with Mr. Scott's recent actions?"

"No… Well, wait a minute. The reason I was fired was

that I corrected some paperwork. I caught the errors and fixed the paperwork before sending it out to the client. Mr. Scott said I sent the client the wrong paperwork but what he'd given me to send had so many errors I had to fix it. I thought he'd appreciate my thoroughness. Apparently, I was wrong."

The sheriff raised the brim of his hat. "Miss Lang, I'd like you to write down your recollection of this event. I know the two of you are getting married in a couple of days but this information might help in our investigation. If you could remember who the letter was addressed to, that would also be helpful."

"I'll do that later tonight before I retire for the evening," Hope offered.

"Speaking of retiring, I best get a move on. My wife will be mighty happy I didn't have to go all the way out to your ranch tonight."

"Good night, Sheriff, and thank ye." Ian waved.

Hope watched Sheriff Bower leave. Ian picked up the reins. "I am glad ye were fired by that man. I would hate to think of ye getting involved, even in a remote way, in all this mess."

"It was a blessing, wasn't it? For months I felt worthless, that I didn't have much to offer but…"

"But ye realized yer worth, and I'm mighty glad ye did." Ian kissed the tip of her nose. "Now, we best relieve Daniel or he will not want to stay on the ranch while we are away for our honeymoon."

"We wouldn't want that." Hope smiled. Life with Ian was going to be exciting.

They made it back to the ranch and within no time Daniel and Mikey were riding back to town in the buggy with her. The number of things she needed to do before the wedding seemed overwhelming, and to add writing an account of what had happened when she'd been fired by Hamilton Scott was not top on her priority list. But she would do it so she wouldn't have to deal with it later.

The next morning she went to the dress shop to finish working on her wedding gown. Along the way, she delivered the account to the sheriff. As she approached the front door of the shop a thin woman with stringy blond hair stood biting her lower lip. "Hello," Hope called out, "how may I help you?"

"Are you the owner?"

"Yes." Hope removed her key from the pocket of her dress. "And you are?"

"Lily Powers. I was three grades behind you in school, Miss Lang."

Hope searched her memory of the younger grades and visually tried to place Lily. "I'm afraid I don't recall you, I'm sorry." Hope put the brass key into the lock and turned it. "What can I do for you, Miss Powers?"

"I'm looking for a job. I can sew pretty well."

"I'm afraid…"

Lily cut her off. "Please, my mother takes in children and, while I don't have anything against children, I'd rather do something else with my life. I figured you'd need someone to give you a hand, since everyone's talking about your dress shop and you making practical work dresses. And since you are getting married…" Lily blushed.

Hope smiled and stepped into her shop with Lily following her inside. "I was going to say I would need to see a sample of your work but I'm afraid I won't be able to do that until after I return from my marriage trip."

"Oh, well, I made the dress I'm wearing." Lily pulled up the hem of her skirt and showed her stitching. "We don't have a sewing machine so I've done all this work by hand."

Hope wanted to hire someone to do some of the sewing, and Lily had a fine hand for stitching. "I'll tell you what. I'll need you to learn how to use a sewing machine. Do you think you can have someone teach you the basics while I'm away?"

Lily nodded yes.

"Good. Then after I return you can show me a sample of your work with the machine."

Lily beamed. "Oh, thank you, thank you, Miss Lang. You won't be disappointed. I promise."

"I'll see you in two weeks."

"Yes ma'am, two weeks. I'll be here with my sample."

Hope smiled and said her salutations. She hadn't meant to give Lily the impression she'd been hired, but if she could master the sewing machine, Hope could use the help. The real question was could she afford it so early in her business?

Hope traced the Irish lace she'd been sewing on the bodice of her wedding dress. The lace was a pattern design her mother had taught her, that her grandmother had taught her. Rumor had it that this pattern went back eight generations. Hope smiled. Perhaps one day she'd be teaching this same pattern to her and Ian's daughter.

Chapter 17

"Hope!" Grace Martin burst through the front door. "We have to— Oh my, your gown is beautiful."

Hope smiled. "Thank you. But that isn't what you came to talk about, is it?"

"No, I'm afraid it won't do to have me as a matron of honor. I'm in the family way."

"That's why you're a matron, not a maid of honor."

Grace rolled her eyes heavenward. Hope laughed then sobered. "Grace, please, you've been through all of this with Ian and me. You've helped me stay focused on the real issues that matter. You just have to."

"But I'm expecting. You know how society feels about women who are in my condition. We are to try and hide it."

"Well, aren't you glad I'm not having a high-society wedding? In fact, there are only a handful of people who will be at the church. The rest will be at the farm for the meal."

Grace walked over to the gown and fingered the lace

collar. "You are going to look stunning in this. And you put in a bustle?"

Hope laughed. "You remember how Ian, when he first came to America, took his dogs everywhere with him and everyone wanted one of his pups?"

Grace nodded.

"Well, that's what I'm doing with this dress. I know there will be gawkers looking on to see what I designed for my wedding gown. Then there are those who are only concerned that Ian and I were not formally courting for a year. But father made it quite clear he reinstated the betrothal."

"Your father is a gem."

"Yes, he is. Well, since you're here, you can help me try this on."

Sally Lang walked into the store. "I'm here. Oh, gracious, ye did a wonderful job, Hope. I'm so proud of ye."

"Thank you, Mum. Come help us put this gown on me."

"Certainly." Sally Lang plopped her purse in one of the chairs and walked over to the changing area.

After fifteen minutes the ladies had the dress on Hope. Hope felt like a princess. "I hope I didn't make this too fancy for Ian."

"He'll love it," Grace supplied and Sally echoed. "Just remind him about how he advertised Tara and Conall. He won't have a leg to stand on." Grace winked.

"Ye are beautiful, darlin'," Sally wiped tears from her eyes.

"Oh, Mum, don't cry."

"I can't help it."

Sally nodded.

Grace looked at Hope. "The two of us are quite a pair. Three, if you count Mercy. I married Richard within three days of our decision to marry. You are waiting a bit longer, what, an entire week?"

Hope laughed. "Yes, a week."

"Mercy held out longer, she waited a month. She also had a bigger wedding. Richard and I were there with Manny and the minister. You'll be having a small wedding but a larger wedding dinner. Richard took me out to dinner at a restaurant."

Hope chuckled. "There was that cruise you went on."

Grace smiled. "One could never forget the sailing voyage we took. Speaking of which, where is Ian taking you?"

"Don't know, he isn't saying."

"I know." Sally winked.

"Where?" Hope stood in front of a mirror, shifting her body back and forth to see the various angles on the dress.

"Nope, I gave me word."

Hope groaned.

"But I know ye will like it." Sally adjusted her hair. "Hair up or down? Ringlets coming down on the side of your face?"

"I don't know."

Grace rubbed her tummy and stepped in front of Hope. "I think up, with small ringlets coming down in front of your ears."

"But Ian likes it down."

"And how much fun will it be for him to take it down," Grace teased. Hope blushed.

Ian worked hard getting the ranch ready for his departure. He left the arranging of the property for the wedding dinner in the capable hands of Mable Sanders, which in many ways was like having his mother here for the wedding. With Mable and Mrs. Lang working on the wedding dinner, Ian didn't have a care in the world about that part.

Even though Ian had been concerned about the addition that Mr. Lang wanted to give them as a wedding present, he was grateful for it. Last night, having seen all the wedding gifts at the Langs' home, he had no clue where they would put all the items. Most of the gifts were coming from Mr. Lang's clients who, even though they weren't invited to the wedding, wanted to express their love and goodwill. This cemented Ian's opinion of the man who was soon to be his father-in-law.

"Ian," Gabe Lang called out as he approached on horseback.

"Gabe, how are ye today?"

"Good." Gabe lifted himself and swung his leg up and over the horse. "Forgive the intrusion but I thought you might need a hand."

Ian noticed that Gabe was dressed in workman's clothes. "Don't ye have a business to run?"

"Not today, or tomorrow. Father decided to close down the office for a three-day weekend. So I'm all yours. What do you need done?" Gabe clapped him on the back.

Ian smiled. "Ye be a good brother."

"Aye, that I am, and don't you forget it. She's my sister and, well, you know."

Ian chuckled. "You'll straighten out this crook in me nose if I don't treat her right."

"You betcha. Tell me what to do, Ian. I'm all yours for the morning."

They worked hard and broke for lunch. "How about a dip in the river?" Gabe asked.

"Sounds refreshing."

Gabe raced ahead. "Last one in is it."

Ian laughed. "What are we, seven?"

"Nope, but I'll still beat you."

Ian sped forward. Being the third son he had to fight and scrape to keep up with his older brothers. Gabe was his age, albeit, he was a city boy. "Good luck, Gabe."

Gabe struggled to keep up. Ian stopped at the water's edge to remove his work clothes. Gabe plunged into him and knocked him into the river. Ian jumped up, madder than he'd been in years. "Ye fool." Ian stomped out of the water.

"What?"

"Me grandfather's watch. It was in me pocket."

"I'm sorry, Ian. Is it ruined? I'm sure if I bring it to the jeweler he can get it working."

Ian calmed himself. Gabe was just being playful and letting off some steam. Tara and the puppies came trailing after them. Ian pulled his grandfather's watch out of his pocket and set it on the bench, which he'd built the day after the house-raising party. "I know ye didn't know, Gabe. I'm sorry for getting so upset."

"No, I would be furious, too. Do you think it will be all right?"

"It's seen worse over the years. But if ye would take it to the jewelers and have him clean it out and oil it, I'd appreciate it."

"I'd be happy to. With any luck he'll be able to do it today for me so you can take it on your honeymoon."

"Thank ye. It was probably in need of a good cleaning." Ian turned and faced Gabe, who seemed horrified. Ian decided in a flash what would break the mood and tackled Gabe down with a splash. Gabe roared, and the two of them wrestled for a bit in the water. It was good to have fun like this.

"You miss your family, don't you?" Gabe sat down in the water at the river's edge.

Ian sat down beside him, enjoying the cool waters washing over him. "Aye, that I do. But I made me choice, and ye and yer sister will make a good family in America."

"Good, because I decided what I wanted to give you and Hope for a wedding present. Now, before you say no, hear me out. I know you purchased a cruise on the St. Johns for her but what I wanted to give you was a round-trip ticket for the two of you back to Ireland."

Ian started to protest.

Gabe held up his hand. "I spoke with Daniel and he's willing to take care of the ranch. I will pay Daniel's salary as part of my gift. Also, I spoke with Mr. Sanders as well as Mr. Hastings. Between those two, Daniel shouldn't have a problem running the ranch. There's a ship leaving for London from Savannah on Monday."

"Gabe, I can't accept that. It's too much."

"Ian, you and Hope need some time alone, private time. What better way than to take a ten-day cruise to Bristol, then a trip on to Ireland, and spend a week or so with your family then another ten days coming back to America? I can afford it. Look at it from my point of view. You are good for my sister. You are encouraging her to use the gifts God has given her and still be your wife. Very few men would do that, especially from our homeland, and you know it."

"Aye, I had to battle some of those notions meself."

"That's what I'm talking about. My sister means the world to me. I want her to be happy and to grow into the woman she's meant to be. I know that her work will take a backseat for a while when she's raising your children. But I believe Hope is the kind of lady who can raise her kids and oversee her business. And I believe you will be encouraging her in whatever she would like to do."

"That I will. But that's a lot of money. I know. I just came here meself."

Gabe placed a hand on Ian's shoulder. "Ian, I have more wealth than you know. I can afford it, many times over."

"I could afford it, too."

Gabe chuckled. "I know what you have in the bank. However, this is my gift to you and Hope. She's special, and I want to give the two of you a gift that will last for years to come. Daniel's willing to stay for two months. That should give the two of you the time you need, plus some."

"I don't know what to say."

"'Thank you' will suffice. Besides, it will give the men Father hired to build the addition more time to get the work done."

"Yer family is too generous."

"We've been blessed and so we like to share the blessings. You'll learn that more as time goes on."

Ian nodded. He'd already seen some of the benevolent behaviors of the Lang family. He had no doubt once he became a member of the family he'd be entitled to know more of their inner workings. "Thank ye, me friend. Hope will be so blessed."

"Good. I'll have Mother pack her trunk with enough clothing for the long voyage. And I'll take care of the various details. You'll need to pack for a month, as well. Do you need some dress clothing?"

"I'll pick up an outfit in town today before we meet with the minister."

Gabe nodded and got up. "I'd better get going."

"Thank ye, Gabe. I'm speechless."

"What's a brother for? Besides, I'm your best man." Gabe winked.

Ian chuckled. "I might have made a mistake there."

Gabe roared. "You'll fit right in, brother."

Ian was overwhelmed and yet grateful to Gabe. What a surprise for Hope. He'd tell her, of course, who paid for the trip, but Ian's mind was working overtime. He would travel home with his new bride. But he would extend the trip a bit, travel through some of the countryside of Ireland. Inside his cottage he pulled out an old book from his sea chest. Inside he found his stash of British sterling. Yes, he would show his bride a wonderful time in Ireland. Ian smiled at the possibility.

Hope worked on the last piece of her going-away outfit, a conservative dress suit with a very slight bustle, similar to the outfit she'd seen in a magazine from London. She'd give Ian the dress to bring to his house so they could change after the wedding dinner. Gooseflesh rose on her arms just thinking of the intimate moment. "Tomorrow, tomorrow," she reminded herself.

She glanced up at the clock. Ian would be here any minute. They were meeting with the parson tonight to go over the ceremony.

She placed the outfit in a garment bag and tied it up with a hanger coming out of the top so Ian could simply hang it in his closet.

"Ah, me love, ye are more beautiful than ever."

Hope turned and found Ian smiling as he leaned against the doorjamb. "You don't look… Have you been swimming?"

Ian chuckled. "Yes, Gabe came by and gave me a

hand and we decided to take a swim after our work was done."

"I hope you won't be offended but I, too, like to swim."

Ian came up beside her and wrapped her in his arms. "I look forward to swimming with ye." He kissed the nape of her neck.

She turned in his arms. "And I with you."

"Tomorrow can't come soon enough." Ian smiled.

"In less than twenty-four hours we'll be husband and wife." She kissed him on the cheek.

He turned his head and kissed her on the lips. A peace engulfed Hope, a comforting peace, a settling peace. She and Ian had made the right decision to marry. She knew it now, and in his arms, she had no doubt. "Ian, I do have a question." Ian stepped half a step back. "I'm wondering about children. How many do you want?"

"As many as the Good Lord gives us. I'm not anxious to have a dozen or so. But probably more than two."

"I'm comfortable with that. I'm glad you don't want a dozen."

Ian chuckled. "I breed sheep and dogs. Children are an inheritance, and they will require more of our time." Ian paused. "Sweetheart, I was keeping our honeymoon as a surprise. But something came up today and I wanted to speak with you about it."

Hope stepped out of his arms. "All right."

"Gabe came by, as I mentioned, and he wanted to give us our wedding present."

Hope nodded.

"He's giving us a trip to Ireland."

Hope's eyes widened. Gabe was a generous man. "Are you wanting to move back to Ireland?"

"No, sorry, a round-trip back and forth from Ireland."

"Oh, my."

"Yes, it is a very generous gift. We will leave Savannah on Monday to Bristol, England. From there we'll take a voyage to Dublin, then a carriage ride out to me parents' farm. However, if ye are agreeable, I'd like to stay longer and show ye some of the other sights in Ireland. Gabriel has arranged for Daniel to live at the ranch and care for the sheep for up to two months. Gabe feels it will give us the alone time we need and haven't been able to have too much of here."

"Gabe is a wonderful brother. I love it. I'll have to repack."

"Gabe is speaking with your mother and she'll help out." Ian stepped closer. "Is this acceptable?"

Hope leaped into his arms. "More than acceptable. We'll have such a wonderful time. And I won't have to cook or clean for the entire trip."

Ian laughed. "True."

Hope pointed to the dress bag. "We'll leave this here while we visit with the pastor then I'll need you to bring it to your house so I can change from my wedding gown to this."

"I can't wait to see ye in both outfits."

"Soon, love, soon. You know, I've been thinking. Isn't it odd that our parents arranged our betrothal not knowing who we would turn out to be, and yet we're a perfect match?"

"Aye, perfect with some growing room. It would have been wrong for us to marry as soon as I came to America. I needed to grow and change."

"And I needed to get over the issue of my parents arranging my life. For so long I resented them for that."

"Aye, me, too. Which is why I think Gabe's gift is wonderful. Me parents will be pleased to see how much we love one another."

"I look forward to meeting them. But more importantly I look forward to being Mrs. Hope McGrae."

"And I look forward to becoming the best man I can be for me bride. I love ye, Hope."

"I love you, too, Ian."

Epilogue

Ian tugged at his collar.

"Stop that," Gabe whispered and nudged him.

Ian mumbled. The starched collar chafed. He had to admit he looked professional in his wedding clothes but he preferred his flannel shirts and open collar much more.

Hope. He focused his mind on the reason he'd dressed this way. She was worth every uncomfortable minute of this strangling attire.

The organist started playing.

"That's our cue. You ready?"

Ian nodded.

Gabe stopped and placed a hand on Ian's shoulder. "You are certain you want to marry my sister? Because if you have any doubt, I don't want my sister married to…"

"I'm certain. I love her, Gabe, more than anyone or anything." Ian bent down and scooped up Clare. He'd given her a bath and brushed her puppy fur. If ever there was a walking fur ball, she was it.

"Let me have her." Gabe reached over and grabbed the pup and held her away from his dark suit coat. "Do you think she'll be quiet?"

"We'll see. I've been working with her all week. She's young but I think she's picked it up. Of course, she's probably gained a couple of pounds with all the rewards."

Ian checked the bow wrapped around Clare's collar and the slipknot that held the gold ring in place. It was risky but he hoped it would give Hope an extra memory. He kissed the top of Clare's head. "I can't believe I'm going to allow a dog to be a pet."

Gabe chuckled. "I doubt this will be the last one."

The organ music grew louder.

"Come on, or the pastor will come searching for us," Gabe said and carried the pup behind his back.

Ian stepped out. The church was nearly empty, just a small group of close friends and family. The wedding dinner would be huge but this…this was what Hope and he wanted. He took his appointed place.

Gabe stood beside him and angled his body to hide Clare. Ian smiled and gave Clare the hand signal to remain still and quiet.

The organ music shifted. The few attendees stood. Grace Arman came down the aisle. She beamed and gave him a wink.

Then his eye caught a flash of white silk. His heart thudded in his chest. His smile brightened. "Oh my," he gasped.

Hope caught sight of Ian. His face burst into the brightest, most joyous smile she'd ever seen on him. And she'd seen quite a few. She fixed her eyes on Ian and walked down the aisle.

It seemed to take both forever and just moments. But then she was there beside him. Being so close to Ian she ached. How could she love him so completely? And yet she did. Confidence filled her to overflowing. He winked. A swarm of butterflies fluttered in her stomach. Her knees started to buckle, and her father wrapped his arm around her waist.

"Who gives this woman to be married to this man?"

"I do," Drake Lang said, then lifted his daughter's veil and kissed her on the cheek. "Her mother and I do." He whispered in her ear, "We love ye."

Hope's eyes watered. "I love you, too."

Ian stepped over and reached out his hand.

Hope took it and stepped up on the chancel and stood with her soon-to-be husband in front of the pastor. He spoke of marriage, of the commitment to one another, and of their need to be open and honest. Then he asked, "What symbol do you give as a token of your love and commitment?"

Ian reached behind him to Gabe, who moved awkwardly. "This ring...and Clare."

Hope gasped, and her eyes spilled over with liquid joy.

Those in attendance laughed. She gave her bouquet to Grace and took the pup. There was a bright red silk bow wrapped around Clare's collar.

Ian untied the ring and placed it on Hope's finger.

She held Clare close. "Is she really mine?"

"Yes, me love."

She leaned over and kissed him.

The pastor cleared his throat. "I haven't given you permission to do that yet." He winked and chuckled.

"Sorry." Hope snuggled Clare and leaned into Ian's embrace.

"By the authority given to me by the Lord Almighty and the laws of this state, I now pronounce you husband and wife. You may *now* kiss the bride."

Ian wrapped her in his arms. Clare wiggled free and jumped down. Hope didn't care, not now, not at this moment. She caressed Ian's face. "I love you."

"I love ye, too." He closed his eyes. She did the same and the warmth of his lips calmed her. They were one.

Hand in hand, they turned toward the congregation and walked down the aisle and into their future with Clare prancing behind them.

* * * * *

REQUEST YOUR FREE BOOKS!

2 FREE INSPIRATIONAL NOVELS
PLUS 2
FREE
MYSTERY GIFTS

Love Inspired®

YES! Please send me 2 FREE Love Inspired® novels and my 2 FREE mystery gifts (gifts are worth about $10). After receiving them, if I don't wish to receive any more books, I can return the shipping statement marked "cancel." If I don't cancel, I will receive 6 brand-new novels every month and be billed just $4.74 per book in the U.S. or $5.24 per book in Canada. That's a savings of at least 21% off the cover price. It's quite a bargain! Shipping and handling is just 50¢ per book in the U.S. and 75¢ per book in Canada.* I understand that accepting the 2 free books and gifts places me under no obligation to buy anything. I can always return a shipment and cancel at any time. Even if I never buy another book, the two free books and gifts are mine to keep forever.

105/305 IDN F49N

Name _____ (PLEASE PRINT) _____

Address _____ Apt. #

City _____ State/Prov. _____ Zip/Postal Code _____

Signature (if under 18, a parent or guardian must sign)

Mail to the **Harlequin® Reader Service:**
IN U.S.A.: P.O. Box 1867, Buffalo, NY 14240-1867
IN CANADA: P.O. Box 609, Fort Erie, Ontario L2A 5X3

**Are you a subscriber to Love Inspired books
and want to receive the larger-print edition?
Call 1-800-873-8635 or visit www.ReaderService.com.**

* Terms and prices subject to change without notice. Prices do not include applicable taxes. Sales tax applicable in N.Y. Canadian residents will be charged applicable taxes. Offer not valid in Quebec. This offer is limited to one order per household. Not valid for current subscribers to Love Inspired books. All orders subject to credit approval. Credit or debit balances in a customer's account(s) may be offset by any other outstanding balance owed by or to the customer. Please allow 4 to 6 weeks for delivery. Offer available while quantities last.

Your Privacy—The Harlequin® Reader Service is committed to protecting your privacy. Our Privacy Policy is available online at www.ReaderService.com or upon request from the Harlequin Reader Service.

We make a portion of our mailing list available to reputable third parties that offer products we believe may interest you. If you prefer that we not exchange your name with third parties, or if you wish to clarify or modify your communication preferences, please visit us at www.ReaderService.com/consumerschoice or write to us at Harlequin Reader Service Preference Service, P.O. Box 9062, Buffalo, NY 14269. Include your complete name and address.

LIDIR13R

REQUEST YOUR FREE BOOKS!

2 FREE INSPIRATIONAL NOVELS
PLUS 2
FREE
MYSTERY GIFTS

Love Inspired.
HISTORICAL
INSPIRATIONAL HISTORICAL ROMANCE

YES! Please send me 2 FREE Love Inspired® Historical novels and my 2 FREE mystery gifts (gifts are worth about $10). After receiving them, if I don't wish to receive any more books, I can return the shipping statement marked "cancel." If I don't cancel, I will receive 4 brand-new novels every month and be billed just $4.74 per book in the U.S. or $5.24 per book in Canada. That's a savings of at least 21% off the cover price. It's quite a bargain! Shipping and handling is just 50¢ per book in the U.S. and 75¢ per book in Canada.* I understand that accepting the 2 free books and gifts places me under no obligation to buy anything. I can always return a shipment and cancel at any time. Even if I never buy another book, the two free books and gifts are mine to keep forever.

102/302 IDN F5CY

Name _____ (PLEASE PRINT) _____

Address _____ Apt. # _____

City _____ State/Prov. _____ Zip/Postal Code _____

Signature (if under 18, a parent or guardian must sign)

Mail to the **Harlequin® Reader Service:**
IN U.S.A.: P.O. Box 1867, Buffalo, NY 14240-1867
IN CANADA: P.O. Box 609, Fort Erie, Ontario L2A 5X3

Want to try two free books from another series?
Call 1-800-873-8635 or visit www.ReaderService.com.

---

* Terms and prices subject to change without notice. Prices do not include applicable taxes. Sales tax applicable in N.Y. Canadian residents will be charged applicable taxes. Offer not valid in Quebec. This offer is limited to one order per household. Not valid for current subscribers to Love Inspired Historical books. All orders subject to credit approval. Credit or debit balances in a customer's account(s) may be offset by any other outstanding balance owed by or to the customer. Please allow 4 to 6 weeks for delivery. Offer available while quantities last.

Your Privacy—The Harlequin® Reader Service is committed to protecting your privacy. Our Privacy Policy is available online at www.ReaderService.com or upon request from the Harlequin Reader Service.

We make a portion of our mailing list available to reputable third parties that offer products we believe may interest you. If you prefer that we not exchange your name with third parties, or if you wish to clarify or modify your communication preferences, please visit us at www.ReaderService.com/consumerchoice or write to us at Harlequin Reader Service Preference Service, P.O. Box 9062, Buffalo, NY 14269. Include your complete name and address.

LIHDIR13R